STALKING MAGIC

KATE RUDOLPH

GUARDED BY THE SHIFTER

Werewolves. Bodyguards. Mates.
The origins of these shifters are shrouded in mystery,
but they're determined to protect their mates from
any harm that comes their way.

Hunting Season
On the Prowl
Stalking Magic

ABOUT STALKING MAGIC

He's too much trouble.

When Vi picks Leland Rowe up after he's spent a night in a jail cell, she knows he's trouble. He's the last man she wants as a bodyguard. But her coven leader insists. Their coven needs protection and Rowe is the man for the job. One thing's certain, she won't fall for the infuriating shifter. He's riding the edge of danger and dancing with a death wish. He can't be her mate.

She's a brazen witch.

Rowe's wolf stands at attention the second he sees Vi, and that's not the only thing standing. She makes him feel things he's never felt before, and though she riles him up, he wants to leave his mark on her. Forever. He's seen two of his packmates meet their mates. Is it his turn?

He'll never have a chance to find out if he can't keep her safe from a rival coven. Rowe is no match against magic, but he'll find a way to do the job. No matter the cost. He's finally found someone worth living for, but he'll have to risk it all to keep her.

CHAPTER
ONE

"Are you doing alright?" Owen asked it with the kind of caring grin that made Leland Rowe want to groan and sink to the floor.

Considering the floor was covered in shattered bar glasses and vomit, standing was the better option. He hated working weddings. At least this one was over and the bride and groom were on their way to Hawaii for a honeymoon far away from their crazy families.

He wished he could join them.

"I'm fine," Rowe said, brushing a bit of ice off one shoulder. He'd dodged most of the epic beer spill, but the stench invaded his senses.

Owen hummed and Rowe braced himself for whatever his teammate and fellow werewolf—pack-mate? that still felt weird to think—was going to say to him next. The man was too damn optimistic and caring for anyone's good. How had he survived the Army without having all that optimism stripped from him?

Chipper bastard.

"Stasia's picking up dinner. Want to join us? We always have plenty." He patted his jacket and reached inside a pocket to pull out his phone. "I'll update Gibson about the job."

"Thanks for the invite, but I think I'm just going to head home. Enjoy dinner." Rowe had spent the last four days with Owen, and there was a slight, *slight* chance he would murder the man if he had to spend another few hours with him.

Owen shrugged. "Okay, I'll see you later."

Rowe didn't know whether or not to be offended that Owen didn't try and argue him out of leaving. He probably needed to get his head checked. One more fucked up thing about his fucked up existence.

He got out of the building as fast as possible, grateful to no longer be breathing in the disgusting stench of vomit. The sidewalk was slightly less crowded than usual. The work crowd hadn't let out yet, but Rowe walked fast anyway. They'd be coming soon and he wanted to beat them to the train.

He'd only walked for a few minutes when his phone rang. And he would have ignored anyone except for the man calling.

"Hello, major." He was *so close* to the subway. He

only hoped he wasn't about to be sent on another vomit encrusted job.

"Owen let me know the job is finished up," said Jericho Gibson, Rowe's boss and the man in charge of their weird little band of werewolves.

"Yeah, we're all good." He tried to keep his voice neutral. He just wanted this day to be over with.

"Are you doing okay?" Gibson sounded concerned.

Fuck. Rowe took a deep breath, and that was a mistake. The streets of New York didn't exactly smell pleasant. But he worked through it. He'd smelled much worse. "I'm fine. Looking forward to a good night's sleep." That sounded good, right?

"No nightmares?" the major prodded.

"Not for a while now. I'll let you know if that changes." Not that he wanted anyone digging around in his head, but assurances like that were the quickest way to get Gibson off his back.

"Be sure that you do. Rest well. And keep out of trouble." He hung up and Rowe was left glaring at his phone.

What was everyone's problem? Rowe did his job. He showed up to every assignment and no one had any complaints about his work. What did it matter if he went out in his free time? He couldn't even get drunk.

What havoc could he cause?

He shoved his phone in his pocket, tempted to

turn it off. But emergencies happened when he did that, and he wasn't about to tempt fate.

Fate had fucked him over enough, thank you very much.

The train came and he stepped on, glaring at a passenger who shoved his way past him.

Asshole.

The miasma of scents and bodies all pushed together made Rowe's inner wolf want to growl. He hated being caged, and there was no worse place in New York than underground on the subway. It was crowded, tight, and it smelled.

He was made for the forest.

Rowe took shallow breaths and told his wolf to shut his trap. He was a normal man and he could ride the normal fucking subway without a fucking panic attack.

But when he got to his stop, *he* was the asshole shoving his way off the train as fast as he could and speed walking up the stairs to the street. He needed fresh air and space, or the best approximation of it he could get.

Why the fuck did he live in New York?

Gibson wanted him to rest. The team expected him to fuck up. Rowe knew that he *should* go back to his shoebox of an apartment and stay there until it was time to go back to work. That would maybe reassure his people that he wasn't about to go off the deep end.

He considered it, he really did. He wanted to be a team player, whatever that meant. He didn't want his friends to worry about him.

But if he locked himself inside that night, he would go crazy. Simple as that.

So instead of heading up to his apartment, he took a turn at the entrance to his building and went to the garage he paid two arms and half a leg for. His motorcycle was sitting right where he left it, shiny and red and ready to rumble. It was an indulgence, and a stupid one at that. If he was still a normal human…

But he had left humanity behind a while ago.

Now he could ride his bike all he wanted.

It wasn't that werewolves were impervious to harm. Cuts still bled. Bruises still hurt. But they healed *fast*. Except from silver, and that wouldn't be an issue on the bike.

He climbed on and listened as the engine purred.

Oh yes, this was exactly what he needed.

Rowe roared out of the parking garage and down to the crowded New York streets. He didn't know how people with cars did it. He scowled every time he got stuck behind someone and was tempted to ram into them.

Insurance premiums were already a bitch and he wasn't going to take on any more.

He slipped between cars and let out a triumphant laugh as angry drivers honked at him. This was almost as good as running in his other skin. But he wasn't crazy enough to do *that* in the city. At least not during rush hour.

The highway was just as crowded as the surface streets, but Rowe managed to slip between cars and ride the shoulder with ease. He knew it was illegal, but he didn't care.

At least not until flashing lights behind him warned of trouble.

Not today.

Instead of doing the sane thing and pulling over, Rowe sped up. He could already hear Gibson screaming at him, but he didn't care. Consequences were for tomorrow.

Rowe took an exit and swerved at random. He'd traveled past several streets before he realized the cop wasn't behind him.

Huh. That had actually worked?

He kept going, the roads a little emptier now. It took a minute to orient himself, but he realized he was near one of his favorite bars.

That was fate if he'd ever heard it.

Rowe parked the bike and went inside with a bit more swagger than was necessary. The place smelled like spilled beer and regret, and it was a sign he should turn around and go home. He couldn't get drunk. That was something his wolfishness had robbed from him.

Some might have said that Rowe used to like his

drinks a bit too much. Still, he would have rather chosen to quit on his own terms.

Not that he'd actually quit. He still wasted his money, it was just even more of a waste than before.

"If Matty sees you, he's going to blow a gasket." Selma, his favorite bartender, grinned at him as she poured out two shots and slid them towards a couple of patrons. She wore a tight, cropped t-shirt and had pink streaks in her hair. Rowe had tried to take her home more than once and failed every time.

At least she still liked him.

"Matty can step in glass for all I care," he said with a scowl. He and the bouncer didn't get along, and their last disagreement had almost led to blows. Matty was seven feet tall and broader than a line-backer. Rowe wasn't sure that werewolf superpowers would be enough to handle him.

Selma laughed. "You wouldn't say that if he was on shift tonight."

He grinned back. "No, I would not."

"Usual?"

"You know it." He pulled out his wallet and placed a few bills on the bar. A minute later, she handed him his scotch and soda.

Rowe let her get back to work as he sipped his drink. It was still early and far from busy. The bar could get crowded and stifling on weekend nights, but on a weeknight, he wasn't so sure. This wasn't a place where people who wore fancy suits came for a drink after work. His wasn't the only motorcycle in the parking lot.

There was a woman in tight jeans and a tank top shooting darts in the back. Rowe watched the way her body moved for several moments before picking up his drink and heading her way. Maybe this night wouldn't be a total waste.

She hit near the bullseye, and Rowe made an appreciative sound. She glanced over at him and grinned. Then she winked and threw another dart, this one hitting true.

"Think you can do better?" she asked after retrieving the darts from the board.

Rowe held up his hands. "I know a professional when I see one."

The woman laughed. "Would you believe me if I told you this was my first time trying?"

"Absolutely not. I know a swindle when I see one, too." He leaned back against a high top table and sipped his drink. "I think you want to take advantage of me."

Her eyes flicked up and down, taking him in. Then she rolled the darts in her fingers. "Come on, no bet. Just a test of skills."

Rowe couldn't resist. He held out his hand. "Don't make me regret this." He threw a dart and was happy when it hit the board.

"There you go!" The woman clapped a hand over his shoulder. "Here, try it this way." She demonstrated with her own arm before guiding him through the motion.

Oh yes, this night was looking up.

"Hey!"

Rowe groaned. He recognized that shout. He could just ignore Matty. There was no need for violence.

Rowe threw a dart and it bounced off the board and hit the ground.

"Look at me." Anger suffused Matty's words.

Rowe didn't look. He wasn't going to. This didn't need to go south.

"Come on, babe. You need to talk to me. You don't understand—"

Babe? Oh shit. Matty wasn't talking to him.

And his dart partner wasn't thrilled. "I understand perfectly," she said, and Rowe couldn't ignore Matty anymore. He looked between the woman and the bouncer and awareness sizzled in his veins.

Violence hung in the air, and Rowe had to resist. He wasn't going to get into trouble tonight.

Then Matty reached out and clamped a strong hand around the woman's arm. "Come on," he said, trying to tug her away. "One drink."

The woman struggled, but Matty was strong and she couldn't break free. "Let me go. Things are over between us."

"Please, babe." Matty was sounding more desperate by the second.

This wasn't going to go well.

The woman tore her arm away and stumbled back. Matty jerked forward to grab her, and that was when Rowe stepped forward.

"You heard her, Matty. Step away." He tried to keep his tone even. He didn't want to fight. This could end peacefully.

Then Matty glared and pulled his fist back.

Fuck. This was going to hurt.

CHAPTER
TWO

Mystical energy swirled around Vi, and she let it sink into her as she guided it to the coven's will. Rosalie, the coven leader, chanted the incantation. Incense tickled her nose and the energy tickled behind her ear, but she kept still. It had been a while since she'd participated in a ritual like this.

She'd missed it.

Going on tour as a roadie for Mercy, one of the biggest rock stars in the world, had been the experience of a lifetime. But now it was good to be home.

Rosalie ended the chant and pulled all the magic toward herself before it released with a shock of power that broke the circle. Vi stumbled back, and she wasn't the only one.

She shot a questioning look at Darnell, but he didn't seem shocked. Apparently, things had changed in the months she'd been away. Rosalie hadn't been that powerful before Vi left.

"You're going to get in," Rosalie told Deliana, the daughter of Delia, one of Vi's coven mates. She was sitting in the center of the circle dressed in all white with a wreath of greenery around her neck. "No school could resist you."

The girl smiled, though she still looked a bit shell shocked. "Let's be realistic. My SAT score wasn't that great."

But Rosalie was shaking her head with an indulgent smile. She stepped forward and led the girl away, all the while reassuring her with comforting words.

"I could have used a spell like this when I was going to school." Mara bumped her shoulder against Vi's. "There's drinks in the cooler." She nodded back towards where they'd parked their cars.

Was it cliché to do magic by moonlight at the edge of the woods? Perhaps. But at least there were snacks. And the sun was already starting to kiss the horizon. This was an early morning rather than a late night.

"When did Rosalie come up with this one?" Vi followed Mara towards the cooler, careful not to trip over the woman's flowy dress. Thankfully there wasn't a dress code. Vi was more of a tight jeans and leather jackets sort of woman.

Mara pulled out two water bottles and tossed one

to Vi. "Last year, maybe? She's had her head in those new books for a while. We've been doing things you wouldn't imagine."

That was certainly true. Though Vi's imagination was expanding all on its own. "Let's just hope she doesn't start summoning magical shadow beasts." Vi shuddered at the memory.

Mara looked confused. "Why would she?"

Right. Vi hadn't been sworn to secrecy after helping out Mercy—Em to her friends—and her new mate, but she wasn't one to spread rumors. "No reason."

"Are we going to need to do one of these for you?" Mara asked.

"What? Why?" Vi could see that Deliana and her mom were still talking to Rosalie and Deliana hadn't taken off the wreath.

"Weren't you thinking about grad school?"

"I don't think that's for me." Once upon a time, Vi had imagined a career in academia, burying her head in musty old tomes and eking out the secrets of the past. Then the realities of school slammed over her and she'd rather be any place but that.

Mara let it go, but only to drop another bomb. "Noah is back in town."

"Is he?" Her voice was even. That was good. She hadn't thought about Noah in weeks. Most days she was sure she was over him. It had been more than a year since the break up. And, coincidentally, about a year since she'd started wandering away from the coven.

So had he. They both needed the break.

She couldn't quite explain what went wrong between them. One day it seemed like all was well. The next Noah was calling her a liar and insisting she was keeping things from him. She knew she wasn't. Everything went downhill from there.

There were worse ways for relationships to end, she supposed. But the failure stung.

Mara kept talking like Vi wasn't reeling. "Yes! Katrina and I had him over for dinner the other night. He's travelled so much. You two will need to swap stories. Between the two of you, you've probably covered half of the world."

"Right." Vi took a deep swig of her water and searched desperately for an excuse to leave. Rosalie caught her eye and nodded for her to come over. Vi made her excuses and went.

Deliana gave Rosalie a hug before she and her mom shuffled off to their car.

"It's good to have you back," Rosalie said. She was on the other side of fifty and had been a good friend of Vi's aunt. Vi couldn't remember a time when Rosalie hadn't been an honorary aunt, and she'd been so happy when she was voted in as coven leader five years before.

"It's good to be back. I missed this." She was a little surprised at how true it was. When Vi had walked away, she was ready to be an independent witch with no need for a coven and the camaraderie it provided.

She'd been wrong.

Rosalie gave her shoulder a squeeze and then tugged her toward the parked cars. Vi followed until they were standing in the small lot, far enough away that they couldn't hear the murmuring voices of the rest of the coven. And no one could hear them.

"Is something wrong?" Vi asked, suddenly worried. Her eyes flicked up and down, taking in Rosalie, but the woman looked healthier than ever.

Rosalie gave her a reassuring smile. "No, no, nothing to be worried about. But there is a... concern... I wanted to discuss with you."

"Of course." Vi leaned against the trunk of Rosalie's old silver sedan and waited.

Rosalie glanced at the rest of the coven as if she was checking to make sure they were still far away. "You know about our meeting next week. You're coming, right?"

"With Audra Palmer's coven?"

Rosalie nodded in confirmation.

"Yes, I'm honored to be invited." Vi had expected to be at the bottom of the hierarchy when she came back, but Rosalie and the others treated her like the worldly witch she was. No hazing here.

"Palmer and I have a... history. She... well, it

doesn't matter. But it means that I don't want us going in unprotected."

"Unprotected? We have magic." Vi let off a puff of fire and smoke, an old parlor trick young witches learned to show off.

Rosalie, unsurprisingly, wasn't impressed. "I'd call in an allied coven for support, but I'm concerned that will only make things worse. Do you have any ideas?"

"Vampires?" The bloodsuckers could be creepy, but they were great in a fight. Something about vampirism made them less susceptible to magic than humans, witches, or shifters.

Rosalie shook her head. "Sunlight may be an issue."

"They just get weak, it's not like they burn up." But her coven leader was right, they didn't want to bring someone with such an obvious weakness.

"No, I don't think vampires. But I think you know someone who will be perfect." Rosalie looked at her expectantly.

Vi wracked her brain, but she wasn't sure who Rosalie was talking about.

"You met one on that music tour," Rosalie prompted.

Vi was already shaking her head. "No, no. Absolutely not. They're a terrible choice." Andre had been a hell of a bodyguard, but he didn't know the first thing about magic. "Andre won't want to leave his mate, and his pack is completely ignorant, not only of the magical world, but of what it means to be shifters. We can't expect them to protect us against a coven."

Rosalie got all cryptic and smiled in a way that made Vi uneasy. "Ignorance has its advantages."

"Does it?"

Rosalie kept smiling.

This couldn't happen. "One shot of power and they'll go down. A single witch almost killed Andre and his mate. A whole coven will flatten them."

"We can prepare them, explain the situation. And I highly doubt Palmer will actually cause them harm. I simply want the… option to defend ourselves if things come to a head."

Vi couldn't win this fight. Rosalie had made the decision before she called her over, that was obvious now. And it wasn't something so egregious that Vi was about to walk away from the coven again. So her shoulders slumped and she nodded. "I'll call Andre and see what he and his people can do."

Rosalie grinned. "It's good to have you back." She kissed Vi on the forehead and walked away.

Vi pulled her phone out of her pocket and glared at it. She hoped this didn't blow up in her face.

CHAPTER
THREE

Rowe hadn't been charged with anything.

Yet.

But he was sitting in a holding cell and glaring at the bars. He wondered if he could shift and use his strength to break out. Probably not. He was a werewolf, not a superhero. And if he shifted while he was in a cell, he was sure he'd either be killed or transferred to some secret government facility to be studied until he died.

He was done letting the government own him. His time in the military was over.

Rowe shifted in his seat. He wanted to get up and pace. He had no idea what time it was or when he could expect to go home. *Were* they going to charge him? Or were the cops just fucking with him?

He was the only guy in the cell, which was a blessing for everyone. He hadn't wanted to fight

Matty, but the already healing bruise on his jaw was proof that he couldn't always get what he wanted.

Now, though? Now he was ready to brawl. But he wasn't so desperate that he was going to punch concrete or steel.

Footsteps echoed down the hall, and a cop glared at him through the bars before unlocking the lock and jerking his head at Rowe. "Get your ass moving. We need the cell."

It was a holding cell. It could easily hold multiple people. But Rowe wasn't a complete idiot and he wasn't about to argue. He followed the guard to the desk and had to sign some paperwork before they shoved his belongings at him.

His phone was ringing.

Rowe wanted to ignore it. He wanted to slink home and lick his wounds. No one needed to know about this little embarrassment. There hadn't been any charges filed. There didn't need to be a record.

But Gibson was calling, and Rowe had the sinking feeling that he knew.

"Hey, boss." Rowe tried to sound cheery and it fell flat. He wasn't a cheery guy.

"What part of stay out of trouble did you not understand?" Gibson wasn't yelling, and that was bad. He was channeling the kind of cold anger that had the tendency to go nuclear.

Rowe opened his mouth to try and explain, but the words got caught in his throat. It would all sound like excuses. Instead, a question popped out. "How did you know?"

Gibson scoffed. "I have friends. Do you?"

A growl threatened to escape, but Rowe held it back. Or tried. When Gibson growled back, he was sure he'd failed.

"Stay where you are," Gibson commanded. "I'm sending you and Hunter on a job. If you fuck this up… *don't* fuck this up."

Before Rowe could make any promises or smart-ass comments, Gibson hung up.

Rowe stared at his phone, wondering if the major would call back. He didn't. A petulant part of Rowe wanted to ignore the order and head out of the station. Hunter would find him, eventually. Hell, she could probably handle the job herself if she didn't have an alleged fuck up like him weighing her down.

Rowe sank onto a bench in the drab, gray hallway and waited for his ride.

He couldn't leave Hunter hanging. She was basically a baby. Well, a twenty-three-year-old, which wasn't any different as far as he was concerned. She was good at ordering pizza after their hunts, but he didn't want her handling a job alone.

So he had to be on his best behavior.

Damn Gibson.

Rowe was supposed to have time off. Jumping from job to job to job led to exhaustion, and Gibson liked to give them downtime. Rowe hadn't even had a full day, and he certainly wasn't counting his time in a cell as R&R.

How much did tickets to Tahiti cost? He was due for a long vacation.

If Gibson didn't tear him a new one first.

Gibson didn't get mad, but somehow Rowe had managed to anger him. At another time he might have been proud of himself. But not today. He needed his job. Not just for the money it provided, but for the contact with the people he worked with.

What would he do without a pack?

He'd been a bit of a loner before, and it had suited him just fine. But these days, something inside of him screamed out for connection. Was he looking for that in all the wrong places?

Maybe.

But at least he was looking.

He didn't know what would happen if he had to make his own way in the world. He wanted to know why he could do what he could do, and the only people in the world who had any information about that were his coworkers, his pack. If he was cut off from that…

But he was getting ahead of himself. Gibson hadn't threatened to fire him. Rowe was just spiraling. And he needed to stop.

Awareness pricked at the back of his mind, and he turned toward the door, expecting to see another cop walk through. But the woman who walked in wasn't like any cop he'd ever seen. She had him sitting up straighter and taking note.

Her hair was dark with streaks of pink and purple in it. Tight, ripped jeans and an old t-shirt covered light brown skin and hugged curves that Rowe wanted to get his hands on. Something wild in him jerked against his hold and he breathed deep, trying to catch her scent. But that was madness. His senses were slightly heightened in his human form, but he couldn't smell a person from across the room, especially not in a place as... fragrant... as a police station.

He wanted to get up, stalk over to her, and back her against the wall while he breathed her in deep and followed it up with devouring her. What would she taste like? Bright, he was sure, and a bit threatening. She looked like the kind of woman who knew how to use a knife. But he still wanted to get closer, wanted to risk the sharp edges of her to find out.

Desire rode him hard. He knew attraction—it was an old friend and had led him to more than one bad decision.

This wasn't that. It was more, and if she gave him the chance, he'd...

Rowe jerked his head to the side and stopped staring. He was in a goddamn police station. The woman was probably a cop or a criminal, and no one he needed to get involved with. He was in enough trouble as it was.

Hunter would be here soon. Hopefully his cock would calm down by then and the memory of the woman would fade.

She was hot. So what? Clearly he needed to get laid if the first attractive woman he saw made him think of conquering cities or some shit like that.

He refused to look her way as her footsteps got closer and her scent enveloped him. Berries and a hint of something spicy. He wanted to roll around in it. He wanted to strip her bare and feast on her until she writhed under him in pleasure.

These fantasies weren't helping his erection subside.

Fuck.

Gibson would kill him if he did something stupid like insult a cop and get thrown back in a holding cell. He reminded himself that he was on thin ice.

His cock didn't seem to care.

He expected her to pass. He was confident enough to know that he looked good on a normal day, but not so cocky that he expected a woman to check him out when he smelled like a jail cell and hadn't showered in two days.

He imprinted her scent on his memory and knew she'd be following him into his dreams, and he looked forward to it. She was a fantasy come to life, and he could do whatever he wanted to her when he slept.

But she stopped in front of him.

Rowe looked up and their gazes locked. A shock of awareness rocked through him as he looked deep into her green eyes. He could sink into them forever. He wanted to.

Who was she?

He needed to find out.

She definitely wasn't a cop.

She took him in, and her green gaze wasn't impressed. She pursed her lips and raised an eyebrow.

"Are you the shifter I'm looking for?"

CHAPTER
FOUR

"What the fuck?" Rowe, the shifter bodyguard she was supposed to be picking up, shot off the bench and stepped into her space. A lesser woman might have backed up. Vi stood her ground. He shot a glance up and down the hall. "Someone could have heard you," he hissed.

"In the empty hallway?" She didn't need to look to see that. Her senses told her enough. Rowe's was the only aura in the hallway beside her. And it was spiky and bright red with desire.

He had dark brown eyes and his pupils were blown wide. His lips were open and begging to be kissed. His chin was covered in stubble that could tip over into becoming a beard if he waited long enough. A desperate part of her wanted to feel it against her body.

He was a few inches taller than her and somehow

managed to loom. She was tempted to send a jolt of magic at him just so he didn't get any ideas, but she was on good behavior. For now.

This was such a bad idea.

His clothes were wrinkled and he could use a shower. This was *not* what she expected out of a bodyguard. Really, picking him up at a police station? What kind of bullshit was that?

She'd done as she'd promised and gotten contact information from Em and Andre, and she'd turned it over to Rosalie. Rosalie, in turn, had instructed her to pick up Rowe and bring him in. But could they trust him? She didn't need some wolf with a screw loose and a chip on his shoulder ruining everything.

That spiky lust in his aura subsided to a dull roar, and Vi's own aura wanted to reach out and roll around in it. It would feel so damn good, and it had been a long time since her aura had reacted like this.

But Rowe was too hot for his own good, and she wasn't going to stroke his ego—or anything else—by giving into temptation.

"Come on." She jerked her head to the door. "Let's get out of here."

She expected him to fight her on it, and he even opened his mouth to say something, but then two uniformed officers walked in and he shut up. As they walked out, she heard the officers talking.

"Some asshole last night decided to play lose the cop. If I see that stupid red bike I'm impounding the hell out of it. Did that idiot want to die?" The woman with red hair tightly held back in a bun glared at the other officer, a man with dark hair and a kind smile.

"So he got away?"

Their voices drifted off before she could hear the answer.

Beside her, Rowe had tensed up, and he walked faster and held the door open for her, rushing down the steps out of the front of the building and waiting for her on the sidewalk.

"Are you the idiot?" The question popped right out. Vi didn't want to care. She didn't want to *know*. It was just one more sign that they needed different support for this job.

Rowe grinned at her. "No comment."

This man was trouble wrapped in a too pleasing package. Vi tried to ignore the spike of lust that shot through her body and flashed out of her aura, reaching out to wrap around Rowe and pull him in.

He shivered and looked at her. "Who are you? What are you? What did you do?"

A shifter should have been able to recognize a witch by scent. Even a child wolf could do it. This was a reminder of just how ignorant Rowe and his pack were. How had they survived this long?

The honking cars around them were her answer. Most shifters abhorred large cities. The sights, sounds, and smells were too much and overwhelmed their acute senses. Living in New York City would be torture.

She wondered how Rowe and his pack did it. And then she shoved the question away. Curiosity would only lead her down a road she didn't want to travel. She didn't care about him, she didn't want him here, and she wanted this job to be done as quickly as possible.

Hopefully, once Rosalie met with these wolves, she'd realize they were unsuited to the job and this would all be a silly memory.

Somehow Vi didn't think she'd be so lucky.

"Come on, I'm parked over here." She hated driving in the city, but sometimes it was necessary. This wolf was sure to have questions.

She drove a black sedan that had seen better days and at least three previous owners. The car was nearing 200,000 miles, but somehow it kept running.

Okay, the somehow was magic. Every time Vi climbed inside, she sent a burst of power through the engine to fix any minor problems that could have crept up. It wouldn't make the vehicle last forever, but she was pretty sure she could get to half a million miles before she had to give up.

Rowe didn't comment about the quality of her car or the dings on the door, and she was grudgingly impressed. Most guys saw her car and had to make a remark. It wasn't pretty but it got the job done, and that was all she needed.

Once they were inside and headed toward Brooklyn, Rowe turned to her. "So what is this job? How do you know I'm a werewolf? Are you?"

She almost, *almost* felt bad for him. He was completely ignorant of his own kind. She'd gotten the story out of Andre when she helped him and Em with their ghost wolf problem a few months back.

Rowe and his pack had all been kidnapped off of a US military base in Germany. They'd been taken into the Black Forest and some "evil wizard" had done magic to turn them into wolves. It hadn't been immediate. They'd all been discharged from the military to hush the situation up, and then a few months later they'd changed on the night of the full moon.

It sounded fake.

First off, no one called themselves a wizard outside of children's books. Second, she'd never heard of a spell that could make someone into a shifter. A bite? Sure, that was easy enough. But magic? Why go to all the trouble? And if you were going to go to all the trouble, why let the wolves go after the fact?

She hadn't dumped those questions on Andre or Em, and she wasn't about to shoot them at Rowe. But she was tempted to dig further. There was more to the origin story of this pack than they understood, and she wanted to uncover it.

But for now, she had to prepare Rowe. "I'm a

witch. I met your friend Andre and his mate on Mercy's last tour."

"You're the one who helped them?"

She nodded. She couldn't look over at him—the streets were too crowded, and she wasn't about to take her eyes off the road for a moment. "That's me. My coven leader asked me to get in touch with your boss for a job. I'm taking you to her now so she can explain things."

"Coven? Those are real? What kind of powers do you have? Do you have a magic wand?" He angled himself in his seat and leaned toward her.

She wanted to look at him, but she still couldn't. Maybe they shouldn't have had this conversation while she drove. "Of course covens are real, I have normal witch powers, and the only magic wand I use has nothing to do with the supernatural."

Oh, she shouldn't have said that last part.

His lusty aura spiked again.

Hers responded.

"Tell me more about the wand." There was an edge to his voice.

His aura felt good. Too good. How was she supposed to resist it when she was locked up in a tight space with him? Her body tightened, and she wanted to reach out and grasp—

A car honked, and Vi realized the light had changed from red to green.

Fuck.

She needed to pay attention. She wasn't going to fuck Rowe, no matter how red and tempting his aura —or his body—was. She drove on and tried to ignore thoughts of wands and werewolves.

"Shut up before I put a hex on you," she warned. "Rosalie will explain what you need to know."

CHAPTER
FIVE

Rowe wanted this tempting witch in his bed. He was determined to have her. She was doing something to him, making her scent more intense, and it spiked his lust every time. He wanted to breathe her in until there was nothing but her scent, and he wanted to find a way to mark her so everyone knew she belonged to him.

What the fuck?

Rowe shook his head and tried to rattle the thought free. It was one thing to want to fuck. That was normal. Natural. But what was this bullshit about marking? He didn't need the prickly witch to belong to him.

She's mine.

The thought whispered through his head, a temptation almost too hard to resist. Almost. Rowe didn't need weird thoughts like that jerking him around. If he wasn't careful, he was going to start acting like Owen or Andre.

And that wasn't Rowe's style. He wasn't looking for forever. One night—or a nice long weekend—was more than enough for him.

Something inside of him was unsettled at the thought. Strangely, it felt like his wolfy self. But Rowe ignored it. He was a human, he was in control.

He didn't need strange wolfy magic interfering with his decisions.

Vi found a space on a street in front of a brick apartment building in Brooklyn. They walked up three flights of stairs and she knocked on the door of apartment 3A. Rowe heard movement inside the room, and a moment later an older woman, in her fifties or so, opened the door and smiled at both of them.

"You found him," she said to Vi.

Vi grumbled something that wasn't quite words, and the woman laughed.

"Come in," she said. "I'm Rosalie Sutton."

The apartment was clean and fairly large. The living room had a sectional couch that could seat more than five people, ten if they squished in. There was a large TV hanging on the wall and another wall had a large window that looked out over the city. The kitchen was small but open, and there was a two-seater breakfast table off to one side.

Willa Hunter was seated at the table and had a glass of what looked like orange soda in front of her.

"Would you like something to drink?" Rosalie asked.

Rowe's stomach growled. He hadn't eaten since… shit. Since before he hit the bar. And one thing he knew was that wolfy metabolism was much faster than regular metabolism. He felt a bit nauseous as he realized just how hungry he was. But he didn't want to ask for food. He was wary of drinking anything she offered. She was a witch. What if she did magic on it?

Rosalie grabbed a small bowl that was already filled with nuts and placed it on the table by Hunter. Hunter pushed the bowl in his direction.

He wasn't fooling anyone.

"A water would be fine, thanks." She wanted to hire them. Why would she do magic on them? Still, he watched her like a hawk as she grabbed the glass from a cabinet and filled it up from the tap. When she handed it to him, he drank cautiously.

Then he reached for the nuts and realized he'd already eaten more than half of them.

Fuck it.

He ate the rest. If he was going to get spelled, it was already too late. At least the nuts took the edge off his hunger.

"Why do you smell like… that?" Hunter

scrunched her nose up and looked at him questioningly.

"I'll tell you later," he promised and hoped she would forget.

Vi sank down onto the couch and Rosalie leaned against the kitchen wall. "Thank you both for coming on such short notice. I've heard a lot about your team and I think you'll be just what we need."

"Can you lay it out for us? Gibson didn't give me much detail." Hunter sipped her soda and sounded so innocent that Rowe wondered why she hadn't gone into sales or become a con-woman. She had the disarming attitude for it.

She was young. Maybe when it was time to switch career paths, he'd mention it to her.

"We are going out this weekend to meet with a rival coven. It's essentially a business meeting and I don't expect much violence. But, well, we have a history, and I'd like to be safe. We'll arrive at the site on Friday night and leave Sunday night. I'll want the two of you present the entire time. You'll ensure that the other coven doesn't do anything untoward, and that no one disturbs our meeting. It's simple enough."

"That's really more than just the two of us can handle," said Rowe. They'd need to sleep sometime. "I think we should call in more support from the rest of the team. We can work in shifts, give you more coverage."

"Absolutely not." Rosalie's response was swift and

final. "It's one thing to bring in support, but an entire *flank* of bodyguards will make us appear weak."

"So we're ornaments," said Hunter. "You only want us there as decoration, not to actually do anything."

"We don't work like that," Rowe added.

"You need to," Rosalie said, as if she had any power over them.

He and Hunter exchanged a glance, and for some reason, Rowe was tempted to look over at Vi, but he kept his eyes on the task.

"We're done here," he said as he and Hunter stood. "I'm sorry, but I don't think we can help you."

They took two steps toward the door before Vi said, "Rose, come on. Be reasonable."

"We'll give you information about witchcraft and shifters," Rosalie threw out, rather than accepting his terms.

It stopped Rowe in his tracks, and Hunter nearly ran into him. The pack knew next to nothing about magic and barely more about shifters. Until a few months before, they hadn't even known they could transform people into werewolves with a bite. And here was a witch offering exactly what they wanted.

No wonder Gibson wanted him and Hunter there.

"We need to have a backup team on call," Rowe insisted. "If all is well, the other coven won't ever see them. If things go wrong, Hunter or I call them in."

"With my permission."

"No. You want us to keep you safe, we'll do it. But you have to trust us. What do you say?" This was as much as he could bend. He wanted the information that Rosalie promised, but he wasn't going to take a suicide mission.

Rosalie gave up. "Very well. You may alert a backup team and call them in if necessary. But I expect you to use discretion."

Rowe grinned. "I'm always discreet."

Both Hunter and Vi snorted.

Rowe ignored them. "Tell us about the job."

Rosalie pulled out a USB and handed it over to him. "That has supplementary information you can go over later. But for now, please take a seat. Let's get started."

CHAPTER
SIX

Vi watched the door for several seconds after Rowe left with Hunter. Snapping her gaze away took more effort than she cared to admit. What was it about the shifter that made her... curious? She wasn't a damned cat, and she didn't have time to be attracted to a wolf that was made of trouble and a bad attitude.

But that wasn't the biggest issue. There'd been a weird thread through that meeting, something that felt just a bit *off*. And Rowe had a point about protection. What was Rosalie playing at?

She looked to her coven leader, who was tidying the table where the shifter bodyguards had sat. "Why won't you let them have backup? Extra shifters won't make us look weak." She'd heard of covens meeting with whole battalions of backup, and no one gave it a second thought. They were powerful people. They had powerful enemies.

Rosalie set the dishes in the sink and then gave her a *look*. "You don't know that. This is my decision."

Okay, Rosalie was definitely acting weird. She hadn't been like this before Vi left. Of course, she'd always been concerned about the safety of her people and presenting a strong front, but she'd always been willing to hear arguments when people disagreed with her.

And because of that history, Vi kept talking. "Why do you want guards who will be less than useless? If the other coven comes at us with magic, they can't do anything." Another pack might have had strategies for defense, but not one who'd only learned about witches in the last few months. *This* was why Vi hadn't wanted to work with them. She was sure they were competent professionals, but they didn't know about her world.

Rosalie sat at the table. Her voice was serious. "Worst-case scenario, they can be sacrificial lambs. We won't lose any of our people, and that's the important part."

Visceral horror ripped through Vi as an image of Rowe dead from an enemy witch's magic flashed through her head. She fought to keep her expression calm. For some reason, she didn't want Rosalie to know how much that affected her. It was one thing to acknowledge that security guards might be injured or killed in the line of duty, that was a reality of the job. But they weren't there to be sacrificed. That was monstrous.

She croaked out a goodbye and left Rosalie's apartment. She didn't know if she could stand another minute with her coven leader without exploding with rage and disbelief. Who was Rosalie becoming?

Or maybe Vi was blowing this out of proportion. Rosalie had spoken bluntly, but that didn't mean she planned to let the shifters die.

Vi hoped this was all a big misunderstanding.

On the street, she saw Rowe and Hunter standing close. Their faces were serious and they spoke furiously, though she was too far away to hear.

Did they need to be standing *that* close?

The stab of jealousy that went through her made Vi scowl hard. She didn't even like Rowe. And did she need to remind herself that she'd picked him up from a police station a few hours before? He was so beyond bad news. He could stand as close to another woman as he wanted.

But Hunter was a bit young for him, wasn't she?

Vi didn't know how old either of them was. And since they'd all been in the military a few years ago, it meant that Hunter was well into her twenties by now. She'd guess that Rowe was in his thirties. But Hunter had a fragile look to her, something that made her look vulnerable to a sexy guy like Rowe.

Fuck.

She blew out an angry breath, her emotions all in a knot. Was she mad at Rowe for standing so close to Hunter? Did she think he was some kind of predator? Or was she concocting some convoluted story and... she didn't know. She'd woken up far too early to perform that ritual, and she needed sleep. Focusing on a bad news wolf wouldn't do her any good.

She didn't understand why he was stirring up all these feelings in her.

Are you sure you have no *idea?* A traitorous voice in her mind asked.

Vi told that voice to shut up, and she refused to examine the thought any further. She could be attracted to the shifter. She couldn't really stop that. But she wasn't letting it go any farther than that. She wasn't an idiot.

Rowe seemed to sense her staring at him and looked up. Their gazes locked, and an awareness passed through them, sending a shiver down her spine and making that voice inside her head whisper more insidious things.

Vi ignored the voice, but she couldn't tear her gaze away.

Rowe was looking at her like he wanted to devour her, but hadn't yet decided if it was the man or the wolf who was going to do it. She wasn't sure who she wanted to win out in that fight. And she was a little scared to find out what would happen when he decided.

They were two beings circling one another, and they were destined to crash together. She could feel that deep inside of her. She'd never had the gift of prophecy, thank fuck, but some things didn't require magic.

Magic crackled in her veins, and she wanted to flash it, to demonstrate that she wasn't some easy mark. She had power of her own. But she wasn't about to do that on a public street.

Maybe if he understood her power, he wouldn't be standing so close to Willa Hunter.

That unjustified spike of jealousy was enough to make her look away. And it was just as well. A yellow taxi pulled up, and he and Hunter got in and drove off.

She stayed where she was for another minute, trying to get her emotions under control. She didn't like Rowe. He was stupidly hot, and that was completely unfair. She didn't need the entanglement that would come from getting mixed up with him.

Vi needed to get a grip. Rowe wasn't hers.

And she didn't want him anyway.

CHAPTER
SEVEN

No one was in the office when Rowe and Hunter got there, but that wasn't surprising. They kept the space so they had a place to meet potential clients and congregate if they needed it, but their work mostly kept them in the field.

Rowe was trying to wipe Vi from his mind. He couldn't afford to get hung up on the witch. But the way she looked at him had his cock taking attention. He wanted her.

He couldn't have her.

She was a client, and that was bad enough. Of course, Owen had fallen for a client and that had worked out well for him. But Rowe wasn't worried about *falling* for her. This was nothing more than his cock paying attention. And as long as he didn't act on it, his cock would get distracted by someone else soon enough.

Are you sure?

Rowe growled, his wolf rumbling under his skin. He didn't have time to get twisted up over Vi.

"You okay?" Hunter asked. She was setting up the projector so they could watch whatever Rosalie had given to them together.

"I'm fine," he bit out.

Hunter snorted. "You can go back and talk to that witch you were drooling after. Really, it's not like there's a ton of research to do before we head into a job without any backup." The sarcasm dripped off of every word.

"I wasn't drooling. And get this shit set up, Gibson's going to want a report." He was harsher than he should have been, but Hunter didn't flinch. She was used to the sometimes volatile moods of her coworkers.

She smacked the projector a few times when the computer wouldn't sync, and it took long enough that Rowe was about to offer help, when finally the video resolved on the screen.

"Holy shit," said Hunter.

Holy shit, indeed. Rowe leaned forward to make sure he was seeing what he thought he was seeing. He'd been in the military long enough to see some fucked up shit, but this was something else. It was a body, but all its skin had been removed and all of the internal organs were exposed to the light.

Then the pile of flesh moved.

It wasn't like a zombie. There was no threat from the squirming pile of meat. It was all pain. And a threat. You didn't do that to someone unless you meant business.

A bright flash of light blanked out the screen for a moment, and in a blink, the flesh was blackened and unmoving. The video ended.

"That's *real*?" The question burst out of Hunter, and she swallowed hard.

"Is there an explanation? A supplemental file?" Sickness swam in his gut, but he was determined not to show it.

Hunter leaned in closer to the computer and scrolled through the information, finally pulling something up. "It says that the body was discovered on the edge of coven lands two months ago. There were magical traces that indicate the spell was performed by the same coven who Rosalie and her witches will be meeting with. The head of that coven is named Audra Palmer, though the file doesn't indicate whether or not she did this."

"Go to the next file." Rowe braced himself.

Hunter took a deep breath before she clicked.

Because he was expecting it, it wasn't as bad. But there were a *lot* of bodies, not all of them human. For some reason, the dead animals were worse. Each video came with a report indicating trace elements of magic from Audra Palmer's coven. There was no indication of how they'd determined that, but for now Rowe was willing to believe the reports didn't lie.

Whoever had done this was a monster. And they had it out for Rosalie and her people.

Vi was in danger.

Under his skin, Rowe's wolf bristled. *Protect.* The thought ripped through him, and he had to grip the armrest of his chair to keep from doing anything stupid like running out of the room to kidnap her and keep her somewhere safe forever.

What the hell was wrong with him? He felt possessed.

"There's a list of missing people and damaged property," Hunter said as she scrolled through the files, not paying any attention to his freak out. "Seems this goes back at least three years."

"Do we know why Rosalie wants her people to meet with Palmer's?" If he had this kind of intel on someone, there was no way he'd let his people get close.

"Negative."

Well, that was just too damn much to ask. "Any info about how to defend ourselves against magic? There's no telling what these witches can do." He shivered as he imagined fire shooting out of magic wands.

The only magic wand I use has nothing to do with the supernatural.

Remembering that had his cock surging back to

life, despite all the fucked up imagery around him. Rowe had to push that thought to the back of his mind and bury it under tons and tons of old memories before it made him do something idiotic.

"I'll look through the files. There's a bunch here." Hunter clicked a few buttons and another video popped up on the projector.

"You better make a copy for Gibson. He needs to know what we're walking into."

This job was a bad idea. But there was no way Rowe could walk away.

CHAPTER
EIGHT

Vi didn't recognize these woods. It was dark, but the moon was high overhead, and she had plenty of light to see by. Leaves crinkled under her feet as she moved, and the air was pleasant against her skin.

Her nearly naked skin.

She looked down to see her white shirt was torn to hell and her skirt was in tatters. She wasn't wearing underwear.

And she wasn't awake.

It was almost a relief to realize this couldn't be real. She let herself sink into the dream world. Everything was a bit hazy as she picked her way down the trail. There was no urgency in this dream, nothing but the need to soak in the night and let the wind flow through her hair.

In the distance, a wolf howled, and Vi's heartbeat kicked up.

The impulse pounded through her and she ran. The dirt of the ground was hard against her feet, but she didn't stop. *He* was coming. And he was going to devour her. Twigs broke against her face and she was bound to have scratches. Even worse, she was leaving an easy trail for him to follow.

But she didn't slow down. It would take too much time to move cautiously.

And in the end, she wanted to be caught.

The moon suddenly went dark. Vi blinked, and when she opened her eyes, it was pitch black. She might as well have kept them closed.

Taking another step forward was as risky as standing still. She was tempted to use her magic to cast a lighting spell, but if she couldn't see, neither could he. And she wasn't going to shoot up a beacon and give away her location.

A wolf howled again. Closer this time.

And before she could decide whether to move or not, she felt a presence right behind her. Hot breath on her neck, the air vibrating as it pulsed between the two of them.

She wanted. She wanted so bad she had to bite back a moan and the urge to beg.

Fingers traced up her arm, and she shivered. She thought she felt the faintest trace of claws, but she couldn't be certain. She tried to look down, but the darkness made it impossible to confirm.

She covered his hand with her own, running her

fingers over his joints until she pricked herself on the sharp tip of the suspected claw. It wasn't real. It couldn't be. Shifters were only supposed to have two forms, nothing in between.

But maybe Vi didn't know everything.

He was gentle when she flinched away from his claws, and she was more fascinated than scared. Somehow, she knew that he wouldn't hurt her.

Of course not. He was her…

She wouldn't think it, not even in a dream.

Lips teased her neck, and Vi leaned back into them. His hand came to rest on her stomach, holding her close as he left his mark. A primal part of her psyche wanted him to bite her, to show everyone just how closely they were bound.

She turned in his embrace and sealed her lips against his before she could make that sort of reckless demand.

It was a perfect mistake. Her body wanted to surrender to his. Desire flooded through her, and the wisps of clothing still covering her were a tantalizing promise rather than any kind of barrier. If it weren't for those claws of his, she'd wish he was doing more with his fingers.

And if it weren't for the darkness, Vi would have to acknowledge that she knew exactly who she was kissing. She knew exactly whose hard cock brushed up against her. She knew exactly who held her like he'd fight the world before he let her go.

But dreams were meant for self-delusion.

The next time she felt his fingertips, the claws had disappeared, and he cupped her ass. She made a startled sound against his mouth and his tongue swept in.

More.

She couldn't say it out loud, but that didn't matter. He knew what she wanted, what she needed.

They ended up on the ground, the darkness still surrounding them, but it provided a special kind of intimacy that Vi didn't want to give up. Her dream lover kissed a path down her body, her clothes magically dissolving until she was naked beneath him.

He worshiped her, teasing her nipples and caressing her sex until she was a writhing mass of desire. But she didn't dare say anything, afraid it would somehow break the spell of the dream. And that was something she wouldn't sacrifice.

Not until she had everything she wanted.

But the blaring sound of her alarm clock wrenched her out of the dream and into the dim light of her room, her sheets tangled around her and her body crying out for more of Rowe's touch.

Damn it.

She wanted to pretend it wasn't him. She hadn't seen her lover. It could still be true. But even as she thought it, she knew what was real and what wasn't. She'd felt every inch of his body. She'd touched him. She'd tasted him.

She didn't need eyes to tell her what her other senses screamed at her.

She wanted the shifter. And her body was going to torture her until she had him. But Vi had never been a creature who withheld things from herself out of spite. She reached into her bedside drawer and pulled out the wand she'd told Rowe about.

There was no way she'd tell him about *this*.

But she'd been pulled out of the dream before her body got what it needed, and while she couldn't fix the desire in her mind, she could at least give herself satisfaction.

The wand buzzed to life.

That was one way to start a morning.

CHAPTER
NINE

"Can you really call this a campsite?" Hunter asked as they got out of their car and surveyed the property around them.

It wasn't camping as Rowe knew it. He could run into the woods and survive for days on nothing but his wits and his claws. But before he'd become a werewolf, he might have had a tent and some basic supplies.

But camping wasn't supposed to involve cabins.

There were rows of tiny houses along a gravel path that led to a large recreation building where the road looped back around to allow a driver to easily turn around.

"I think it's called *glamping*," Hunter offered. She popped the trunk and pulled their bags out.

Just because they could survive in the woods with nothing didn't mean they'd come to a job unprepared. "That word sounds fake. You can probably leave the tent in the trunk."

"No shit." She dumped his duffel at his feet, her own slung over her shoulder. "Rosalie texted that she's in the recreation building."

Rowe picked up his bag and they headed that way. Rosalie and her coven were scheduled to arrive first, with Audra Palmer and her people arriving in the afternoon. It would give Rowe and Hunter time to set up and get the lay of the land before the job really began.

Checking in didn't take much time. Rosalie was busy speaking to two witches that Rowe didn't recognize. He *wasn't* disappointed that Vi wasn't there.

If his wolf could have rolled his eyes, it would have.

He and Hunter each had tiny houses of their own. When Rowe stepped inside of his, he couldn't breathe. It felt like the walls were closing in around him. He reached out as far as he could and his hands didn't quite touch the walls across from one another, but it was close. He opened up the window in the bathroom/living/kitchen area and that made it a bit better.

He wasn't claustrophobic, but a man needed more than a hundred square feet to live. It took him a moment to figure out where his bed was. He thought it would be in a loft, but this house didn't have one.

Then he noticed a seam in one of the walls with a clever hook. When he unhooked it, a queen bed unfolded. It took up just about every square inch of space, but at least he'd be able to stretch in his sleep.

He put the bed back up and found places for his things. He was only a little tempted to set up camp outside.

Okay, more than a little. But he'd give it at least one night before he gave up on the shed he was supposed to call home for the long weekend.

Gravel crunched outside, and he thought it was more of Rosalie's coven arriving. He went outside to scope them out, *not* in the hopes that it was Vi who was driving up. Hunter sat on the stoop of her own tiny house, right next door to him, so he walked the short distance to join her.

A small convoy of SUVs had driven up, and the doors opened simultaneously.

"Do you think they practiced that?" Hunter murmured.

Rowe tried to suppress his smile. "I think Palmer and her people are here early."

"Looks like."

They watched as a handful of people got out of each SUV. Rowe counted ten people, thirteen in total, since someone had to be driving each of the three vehicles. And four of them weren't witches. It was clear from their posture that they were there to guard Palmer's people.

And there was something about them.

"They brought their own shifters." Vi seemed to appear out of thin air next to him, and Rowe did his best not to react.

"How can you tell?" He hated that he couldn't. He *should* be able to. He was the werewolf here. He narrowed his eyes, as if that would give him some sort of insight. All of the people who got out of the cars looked normal. If he passed them on the street, he wouldn't have thought they were anything but human.

They were too far away to get a good sniff of them from across the road. He pulled air in anyway and was rewarded with Vi's scent. Berries and spice that he wanted to roll around in all night until all he could smell was her. And under it all, there was a hint of something. Charcoal? Fire? He wasn't sure, and it tickled his nose.

Was that just Vi? Or was it because she was a witch?

"Witches and shifters have completely different auras," she said. If she noticed him breathing her in, she didn't make a comment.

"Auras?" Yes, he knew he was working with witches, but that sounded a bit *woo* for him. If she brought out crystals, he wasn't sure how he'd react.

"Don't act like you weren't just sniffing me." She pinned him in place with a look.

A bolt of arousal shot through him, and he

couldn't suppress his grin. He was supposed to be focused on the job, not her. "What does that have to do with auras?"

"They're basically a magical scent. Only witches can see them, but there has to be a way shifters tell us apart. Maybe you should talk to..." She trailed off and looked over at Palmer's people. Four of them, three women and a man, were standing in front of the vehicles, their posture stiff and eyes roaming around on high alert. Nothing in Rowe's senses said they were shifters, but they were definitely a protective detail.

So they *were* the shifters.

"Ask him," Vi finally said, pointing to the one man in the group of shifters. He was listening intently as one of the women talked. The woman who was speaking looked to be in charge.

"Or I could talk to the leader," he said, just to see how Vi would react. It made the most sense to speak to the person in charge, yet she hadn't pointed him that way. Was it because the leader was a woman? Vi had no reason to want to keep him from other women.

And yet.

Rowe grinned wider.

Vi made a disgusted sound and walked away. Rowe didn't follow. He knew he'd see her later.

"What was that?" Hunter was still in front of her

cabin, though she no longer sat on the steps. "Care to share with the class?"

"I was just collecting information on the job." He tried to sound innocent.

"Uh huh." Hunter wasn't buying it. He didn't blame her.

"Call Gibson. We need reinforcements." He didn't like that Palmer's coven had brought in four people.

Were they planning something? Or did they see Rosalie's coven as a threat? The images on that flash drive were burned into his head. He wanted an army to defend his charges. But he wasn't going to get one.

"I'm on it." Hunter went back into her cabin.

Rowe watched the new arrivals disperse into their own cabins. This job had just gotten a lot more dangerous.

CHAPTER
TEN

Anticipation hung heavy in the air. Palmer, her coven, and their guards had taken up residence in their cabins and had been keeping to themselves in the two hours since they'd arrived. Rowe watched them as closely as he could, but he was only one man. He couldn't see everything.

He wanted to head into the woods and get the lay of the land. If he were planning an attack, he wouldn't do it out here in the open. No, he'd lure his prey out and take them when they were disoriented.

But he was a soldier and a wolf. He didn't think like a witch.

Vi could give him some more insight, but he hadn't seen her since Palmer had arrived. Probably for the best. She was a distraction, and one he couldn't afford. Not right now.

Under his skin, his wolf grumbled.

At some point, Rowe was going to need to figure out why his wolf was so drawn to Vi. Had she put some sort of spell on him?

Could she turn him into a newt?

He shook his head to clear that thought. He highly doubted that was possible. Whatever was going on, it wasn't magic. It was too visceral for that. He understood attraction, understood lust. But this was primal.

He wanted to stake his claim.

He didn't even know the woman, and yet he couldn't resist.

He was going crazy.

The central building was almost empty when he arrived, but his senses picked up on Vi the moment he walked through the door. She was speaking with Rosalie, and they both looked intense. They stopped speaking when he arrived.

"Is something wrong?" Rosalie rose from where she'd been sitting, Vi following suit.

"I wanted to let you know that our backup will be arriving later today. We can bunk up in our cabins if there isn't more room." Rowe shuddered at the thought of sharing that space with anyone. There wouldn't be enough room to breathe. But he'd slept in worse places.

Something dark passed over Rosalie's features, but she masked it almost immediately, her face a picture of calm confusion. "I didn't give approval for extra guards."

"You did. In New York. They have four, we'll have four. We're just evening the numbers up." He wanted to shake Rosalie and demand to know why she was being so stubborn about this, but that would get him fired. And Gibson would kill him if he lost the shot they had at learning about the magical world.

Before Rosalie could argue any further, the door opened again and two women walked in. One of them was the head guard Rowe had seen earlier, and the other was Audra Palmer, who he recognized from the file that Rosalie had prepared for him.

She was about the same age as Rosalie, with brown skin and straight white hair that fell to her shoulders. She was short, but she had a kind of grace that made her seem taller. She wore a simple blue dress, and her only jewelry was a pendant on a gold chain. There was a serenity to her that made him think she'd be a great yoga instructor. But looks could be deceiving. He remembered those videos, that carnage. Was this woman responsible?

Her guard radiated danger. This was a person who definitely had the potential of doing those dark deeds. But did she have the ability? Magic had caused those deaths, not claws.

She was a head taller than her charge, with sharp cheekbones and blonde hair tied back in a braid that looked tight enough to give her a headache. She wore a discreet radio in one ear and dark clothing that would allow her to slip into the shadows as if she belonged there. Rowe's eyes flicked up and down, taking her in, but it had nothing to do with attraction.

This woman was a threat. And a shifter.

He had questions. He was sure everyone in his pack had questions. But he couldn't ask her, not yet. They were in the middle of a job, and admitting that he knew jack shit about being a shifter was akin to suicide.

The shifter guard gave him an assessing look, and her lips twisted into a scowl.

Did he smell funny?

Beside him, Vi made a grumbling noise, but when he glanced at her, her face was completely blank.

The door opened again, and Hunter slipped in behind Palmer and her guard. The guard glanced back for a moment but then returned her gaze to Rosalie.

"Hello, Rosalie," said Audra Palmer, her voice a soothing balm. "It has been too long since we met."

"Audra, it's a pleasure." Rosalie sounded syrupy sweet and completely fake. "I trust you've settled in?"

"Of course. I always love visiting this meeting place. It's so peaceful. Nora wanted to meet you before the festivities start. What have things come to that we're forced to bring outsiders to these private meetings?"

Rowe didn't need to be a genius to know there was a history between these two and a conversation happening under the surface. Maybe Vi would make it make sense.

"Nora West?" Rosalie asked, looking to the guard, who nodded. "I've heard of you. Your services are quite coveted."

Nora kept her face neutral. "Yes." She didn't add more.

Rowe filed the name away in his mind. He didn't know anything about shifters, but security guards were his business. If she was in the business, Gibson or someone else on their team would know about her.

But what if she only worked for witches? He'd deal with that later.

"This is Leland Rowe, and his partner is Willa Hunter," Rosalie offered. "They're simply here to make sure nothing gets out of hand."

"Your alpha is Jericho Gibson." It wasn't a question, but Nora clamped her mouth shut once she made the surprised statement, as if she was ashamed to show any interest.

Neither Rowe nor Hunter answered her. It was strange to think of Gibson in that way. Sure, he was in charge. They'd thrown the term around a bit, but mostly as a joke. The shifter bullshit all felt fake, even when they felt the moon's pull and ran under starlight in their second skin.

And then Rowe wondered how this woman knew Gibson. Was Gibson keeping secrets? Did he know more than he let on? Or was the team making a name for themselves in a world they didn't yet understand?

He wanted to ask her these questions and more. She was the first regular shifter he'd ever met. He was pretty sure she hadn't been kidnapped and changed by a magic spell. Though, technically, Stasia and Em were regular shifters. They'd been changed by a bite. But they were just as clueless as the rest of the pack.

When the job was done, provided everything didn't go to shit, Rowe was going to hunt Nora down and get his questions answered.

But they had to do the job first.

Rosalie and Audra sniped back and forth for a few more minutes before Audra and Nora left. Rosalie deflated a bit, and Rowe realized she'd been holding herself taller while the other coven leader was there.

She looked tired.

This was going to be a long weekend.

"I need to get the lay of the land," he said. He'd wanted to do it before the other coven showed up, but their early arrival had messed with his plans.

"Hunter, stick with Rosalie until backup arrives. We can set up a rotation schedule then."

Rosalie didn't object this time. "Vi knows the land, she can guide you."

If Rosalie had told him to take anyone else, Rowe would have refused. But an excuse to be alone with Vi? That he couldn't resist.

He pulled Hunter to the side and spoke quietly enough that Rosalie and Vi couldn't hear. "Call me if anything looks fishy. I don't expect Palmer or her people to do anything today, but I don't like leaving you alone."

"We need to make sure they haven't planted any surprises in the woods," Hunter said with surprising insight. "The others should be here in an hour. We'll be fine."

He was tempted to put off exploring until the others arrived, but that just gave a malicious person more time to act. So he and Vi headed out.

She silently led him down a narrow path that went deeper into the forest. The sun was high overhead, but the trees were thick enough that it was dim on their path. It would be pitch black come nightfall.

Rowe's muscles began to relax as they walked, the greenery seeping into his nose, tangling with Vi's tantalizing scent. He wanted to push her up against one of the trees and nuzzle against her, drugging himself on her and nature.

This was where he belonged, not cooped up in the

dense city, his senses under constant assault from sights, sounds, smells, and tastes he couldn't process. Out here, he could breathe.

"Remember that Nora West is working for Audra and her coven," Vi said out of nowhere. She was half a step ahead of him and shot a look over her shoulder, along with that volley.

"Of course." For a moment, Vi's statement made no sense. She couldn't be *jealous*, could she? "You know I'm a security guard, right? I was assessing her as a threat, not as a woman." And when he said it like that, it sounded bad.

"I know why you're here." She whipped around. "But you were looking at her like..."

She trailed off, and Rowe held his tongue. At another time, he might have bristled at anyone feeling possessive about him. But from Vi, he wanted to roll around in the feeling. It was madness. He didn't know this woman. He had no claim on her, she had no claim on him. Even if he'd been leering at West, she didn't have a right to say anything.

But his wolf liked that his mate was jealous.

His what?

He tried to chase that thought, to make his wolf answer for that little tease, but his other half settled quietly into himself, content to bask in Vi's presence.

They stood close. He could wrap his arms around her and have her flush against him in a heartbeat. Would she resist? Or would she surrender to it?

She wasn't stepping back. Her scent washed over him, and Rowe breathed deep. She watched him, gaze intense. Then her eyes flicked down to his lips.

Only for a second. But Rowe was watching her so closely that he couldn't miss it.

Her tongue darted out, wetting her own lips.

Fuck.

He was supposed to be scouting. They weren't that deep into the woods. Anyone could ambush them. But his cock didn't care. Not when he was this close to his… Vi.

"If I didn't know any better, I'd say you were jealous." The words came out roughly.

Vi scowled. "Of course not. I have no claim on you." But she didn't back up.

He needed to put space between them and do the job. He couldn't. "Not brave enough to make one?" he taunted.

She made a frustrated sound in the back of her throat, and he expected that to be the end of it. Then her lips turned up into a grin. "I'm going to regret this."

They weren't promising words, but they were the last he heard as she sealed their lips together in a kiss that sent Rowe's world turning on its axis.

Mate!

He couldn't fight the claim, not as his body surged to life, his arms wrapping tightly around Vi and pulling her close. This was the woman he'd been waiting for all his life. This was what he hadn't known he'd been missing.

He wanted to devour her. He wanted to *own* her. He'd leave his mark and know she was his.

And then she'd mark him and there'd be no question.

His hands itched to tear her clothes off and have her right there. And from the strength of her grip on him, he didn't think she'd object.

All thoughts of the job were gone. She was too close. It was too intense.

Until something knocked into him from behind and sent them sprawling apart.

Vi lay on the ground dazed, and it took all of Rowe's self-control not to crawl over her and keep up what they'd started. Instead, he looked around for an enemy that wasn't there.

"This isn't a ghost werewolf, is it?" he asked as Vi got to her feet.

"No."

The ghost werewolf had been a construct created to hunt Em several months before. Andre had gone to protect her and they'd ended up mated.

Rowe had wondered how his friend could fall so quickly. Now he was beginning to understand the pull. He didn't stand a chance. He didn't want to resist.

"It's magic," Vi added. "I can sense it." She took a step off the trail, and Rowe was quick to catch up.

He wasn't about to let her face any danger alone. He wanted to lead the way, but he let Vi do it without an argument. She was following a trail he couldn't sense. He could only protect her from the physical.

They stepped into an area that looked like it had been cleared by a lightning strike. But fire hadn't ripped through the forest. Instead, it stopped about ten feet out from the center, which was marked by a blackened tree covered in scorch and claw marks.

"That's magic," Vi said. "Keep back." She flexed her hand, and it was covered with bright light.

It was the first time he'd seen her do magic. He wondered what else she could do.

"I'm going to try and sense the source of the power." Vi stiffened her shoulders and stared at the tree. "This is bad magic. I don't like it." Her face was grim.

"Are you sure? There's two whole covens back there who can help." She didn't seem confident. "I don't want you getting hurt."

It had to be dangerous, since she didn't snipe at him. "Two whole covens. And at least one of those witches did this. You want to ask them to take a look?"

She had a point. "Just be careful."

"Piece of cake," she said with bravado.

Her magic flared even more ,and she sent ropes of it to wrap around the tree. It got too bright for Rowe to make sense of after a minute. One minute bled into another and then another. He didn't know how long it should have taken, but Vi's breathing got shallow after ten minutes.

That couldn't be good.

At fifteen minutes, she cried out in pain.

"Vi," he said. He got as close to her as he dared and said her name again.

She didn't react.

"Come on, Vi, snap out of it."

She cried out again, and the power went white bright. But it didn't look like Vi was sending it out. No, it looked like the tree was *sucking* her power into it.

Vi's cheeks looked hollow. She was fading.

He shook her shoulders, and it did nothing. Rowe's wolf felt caged and raged against him. He could feel his body trying to shift, claws growing on his fingers and his fangs dropping down.

He didn't question it. His wolf needed him to save their mate.

He gripped her shoulders, his claws digging into her skin hard enough to break the surface, and he wrenched her back, putting himself between the tree and her magic.

It punched into him, and he almost went down. But he wrapped his arms tight around Vi and took it all in.

He felt like he was burning up.

Were they both going to die out here?

And then the magic flashed and faded.

Vi woke from the spell with a gasp. She broke out of his grasp and stared at him like he'd grown a second head. "I was caught in a magic trap. You could have killed yourself pulling that stunt. It's impossible to pull a witch out without getting stuck yourself."

"And yet you're free." They were both breathing hard. He needed to touch her, needed to know she was safe. "Did you figure out who set the trap?"

She jerked her head from side to side.

Rowe reached out. Vi stepped forward. Once he started kissing her, he never planned to stop.

A piercing scream echoed around them, coming from deeper in the forest.

CHAPTER
ELEVEN

Vi's mind didn't have time to reel as she and Rowe sprinted through the forest down the narrow paths toward the screams. The screams that had gone deadly silent. There was no sound in the forest now except for the whistling wind. The birds and small animals had all been scared silent.

The scream had been gut wrenching.

Vi expected to find a body, or, at the very least, blood. She expected the only reason those screams had been silenced was the finality of death. A finality she had flirted with and somehow escaped.

Because of Rowe.

She didn't have time to think about that. Nothing except a strong jolt of outside magic should have been able to pull her out of that trap. And even then, magic strong enough to break that spell would have been likely to kill her. There was no reason a tackle from a shifter would do the trick.

Not unless there was an even stronger kind of magic there.

But she didn't want to think about it.

It had been one hell of a kiss, though.

They stopped running after a few minutes. Sound could only travel so far through the trees. Vi cast out her magical senses, hoping for *something*, but she was weak from the battle with the magic tree, and her powers felt like they were wrapped up in wool.

"Do you sense anything?" she asked Rowe, her breaths coming in labored. She was a city girl. She could walk for hours, but running was not her style.

Rowe scanned the area around them, face grim. She shouldn't stare, she knew that. But she couldn't force herself to look away from him.

This was *so* not good.

Rowe shook his head. "Nothing." He took a deep breath and shook his head again. For a second, his eyes seemed to glow, as if the wolf that lived within him was exerting its power. But that was impossible.

Damn it.

"We should look around," she suggested. Everything where they were now looked normal. The trees looked like trees. The dirt felt like dirt. It all smelled overwhelmingly green. "There might be more enchanted trees. I want to find a hint of who did that."

"No." His tone was firm.

And kind of hot.

Vi scowled. "Excuse me?" She'd already turned to start looking around, and she had to turn back to make sure she'd heard correctly.

"I said no," he repeated. There was no hint of the man who'd kissed her only a few minutes ago. Now he was all business, the strict security guard who was there to keep her alive, not kiss her senseless. "That magic... tree..." he screwed up his face as if he couldn't quite believe what he was saying before soldiering on, "almost killed you. There might be more surprises waiting for us, and we aren't equipped to fight them. And we need to find out where that scream came from. We go back to camp and regroup."

An argument gathered in the back of her throat and clamored to get out. There was some sort of nasty magic in the woods, a threat to her entire coven. She didn't want to leave it there to fester.

But Rowe had a point. The asshole.

Her face was going to cramp if she kept scowling, but she hated following orders coming from the infuriating man beside her. She hated the way her body was attuned to him. She hated...

No, she didn't hate him.

"Fine." It came out razor sharp. "Let's go back."

Rowe opened his mouth to say something more, but showed more intelligence than she thought he possessed when he shut it and led the way back to camp.

They were farther away than she thought, and it took nearly half an hour to make it back. There wasn't much of a trail to go by, but Rowe walked through the forest like he was made for it.

When they finally broke free from the woods and spotted the cabins, Vi was shocked to see everyone gathered outside of the recreation building. She would have thought that the two covens would be keeping to their parts of the camp until it was time to meet.

She and Rowe didn't need to discuss it. They headed straight for the recreation building to see what was going on. After a moment, Rowe picked up the pace, and Vi had to run to catch up. They were close to the building when Vi smelled blood.

Was that why Rowe was running?

He elbowed his way through the gathered witches, and she followed close behind him. She thought they'd have to fight their way into the building, but the action was happening on a picnic table outside.

"Ellie, it's going to be okay." Audra Palmer clutched the hand of a woman with brown braids and sweat-dampened brown skin washed out from blood loss. A large white bandage covered one of her shoulders, and her face was awash with pain.

She was one of Audra's witches. Vi thought they

might have met at one gathering or another over the years, but she wasn't sure.

Ellie screamed.

Audra sent a soothing burst of magic over Ellie's wound, and Ellie quieted. A little. "Julian is preparing a healing spell," Audra assured her witch. "He just needs a little more time."

"What did this?" Rowe demanded. He tried to take another step closer, but Nora West blocked his path, her face stone hard and assured he wouldn't pass.

He didn't try to go further.

"She screamed and came running out of the woods with her shoulder torn up and bleeding," Delia, one of Vi's coven members, reported. "It's not clotting as it should. She's going to…"

"Silence!" Audra snapped at Delia.

"You're not my coven leader." Delia scowled back.

Vi looked around, but she didn't see Rosalie. She was about to ask where she was when Ellie gasped. "Monster. Magic monster. Woods." Then she started shaking.

Things got even more chaotic after that, but then a man, Julian, judging by the healing potion he was carrying, stepped into the fray.

"Give us space," Audra demanded. "Let me tend to my people."

There was a tense moment where Vi was sure her

coven wouldn't comply. They didn't follow Audra. They didn't trust her. She could cause trouble.

But she was tending to her injured.

"Come on," Vi said to the gathered witches. "Back off. Let them work."

It was enough to make her people comply. Vi met Rowe's eyes, and she saw the same wariness that must be in hers.

Evil magic tree. Violent magic monster. One big forest.

Yeah, things were looking bad.

CHAPTER
TWELVE

Rowe was surprised that Gibson had shown up, but he shouldn't have been. The major wanted to know about the magical world. Coming to a gathering of witches was the best way to do that. Gibson and Owen Myers were acting as backup for him and Hunter.

Good thing they were there.

Tensions had only risen in the hour or so since Audra had banished everyone from Ellie's side. Vi had escaped into her coven to speak with her fellow witches, and it was taking more discipline than it should have not to follow her.

Instead, he briefed Gibson and Owen with Hunter by his side. She added her observations about Ellie's run from the forest, and it lined up with what the witch had said.

"There's more." Rowe kept his voice low. Vi

hadn't told the others, but he wasn't about to keep his team in the dark. "Vi and I were scouting in the woods—"

"That's one of the witches?" Owen interrupted.

"She's—" Rowe had to bite back an instinctive defense. The question wasn't even offensive, so why did he want to bite Owen's head off?

"She's the one who saved Em's life a few months back," Gibson reminded him.

"Don't tell Stasia I forgot the name of the woman who saved her sister's life," Owen begged, but there was a playfulness to it, just as there always was. The man was irrepressibly and annoyingly chipper.

"Anyway," Rowe continued, "we were scouting, and we came across a tree imbued with magic. Bad magic. Vi almost got sucked into it, but I managed to break the spell."

"How?" Gibson asked, eyebrows ticked up slightly. He carried the mantle of authority like he'd been born to it, and when Rowe wasn't on the wrong end of the major's ire, he was glad this was the man who'd become his boss. He didn't know if there was any sort of werewolf bullshit, if Gibson had some sort of magical alpha powers or something, but right now he wasn't fighting it.

And Rowe wished he had a good answer. "I tackled her." He didn't say anything about the kiss or anything about his partial shift. And that part he knew he shouldn't leave out.

But he was still figuring things out. And he wanted to figure them out with Vi.

Before his team had a chance to respond or question him further, a hush fell over the gathered witches as Audra Palmer approached. Her sleeves were wet and there was a dark stain on one of them, a mark of Ellie's injury. But she didn't have the grim face of someone bringing bad news.

"Ellis is healing," Palmer told them. "Julian is looking out for her."

Relief surged through the witches, and even Rosalie's coven seemed happy with the news. It lasted less than a minute.

"It was a trap." Rowe couldn't pinpoint the voice, but it was coming from the cluster of Palmer's witches. "They attacked Ellie."

"How dare you!" That came from Rosalie's coven. "We come in *peace*." Magic crackled in the air, a warning that peace was quickly dissolving and they danced on the edge of violence.

Vi kept quiet about the magic trap. He wondered if she wanted to speak to Rosalie, who was still missing, first.

Where was the coven leader? Her presence would go far to calm her people. But no one else seemed particularly concerned.

The two covens argued back and forth. Rowe and his people were ready to step in if it came to blows, and he could see Nora West and her shifters standing in a similar position. Their eyes met, and she gave him a nod of acknowledgement.

Out of the corner of his eye, he saw two figures moving slowly to them, Julian and Ellie, who was on her feet but moving at a snail's pace.

The witches quieted when they arrived. "I thought we should all hear what happened to Miss Hicks," said Audra.

Tension was still there, but the witches kept their silence as someone found a seat for Ellie and she sat. She winced with every move, but the bandage on her shoulder was no longer wet with blood. She would be fine once she had the chance to heal.

Her voice was hoarse but strong. "I needed to ground my energy after such a long car ride. I informed Nora that I planned to walk in the woods for a few minutes. She wasn't happy about it, but I insisted, and she let me go. I walked for a while, letting my energies settle. Everything seemed normal. Then I thought I heard an animal. I looked around, but didn't see anything. So I explored a bit deeper in the woods. There was something—" she shivered before continuing, "—malevolent all around me. Then I heard trampling footsteps. There was a large blur, and then claws tore into me. I can't describe it, but I'm certain it wasn't natural. I managed to send a bolt of my magic at it, and then I ran. I didn't realize how badly I was injured until I collapsed back at the camp."

"I've seen soldiers do some crazy things despite their injuries," Owen offered with a genuinely caring smile. "Adrenaline is a hell of a drug."

Some of Rosalie's witches glared at Owen for so easily believing Ellie's tale, but Vi wasn't one of them.

"Her scent says she's telling the truth," said Nora. Her crew of shifters nodded in agreement, and she looked over at Rowe, as if she expected him to back her up.

He didn't. He *couldn't*. How could a scent tell lie from truth? Could Nora teach them? He could feel unease permeating his own team. There was so much they didn't know about who they were.

"Why should we believe you?" a blonde witch from Rosalie's coven demanded.

Nora turned her attention to her. "My crew was hired to protect Coven Leader Palmer and her people. I was not hired to lie for them." She stared at the blonde witch until she was sure her point was made. Then she looked to Audra. "You need to call off this meeting. The monster in the woods needs to be dealt with. It's too dangerous to stay here."

"I agree," Gibson said from behind Rowe.

All of the shifters were nodding.

All of the witches refused, even Ellie Hicks.

And then the argument started up again. Rowe sat back and listened. He'd do the job, whatever that meant, but no matter what, he wasn't letting that monster… or the magic tree… hurt Vi. He wanted to stand beside her and assure himself he was okay, but that would be akin to making a declaration.

He barely knew her.

They'd kissed once.

And yet his wolf whispered in his head. *Mate.*

"We hunt the monster," Audra's voice rang out above the witches, power crackling in every word. She was a powerful woman, and Rowe knew it would be a danger to cross her. "And here and now, we swear a binding oath to do no harm to one another until dusk tomorrow. That will allow us to focus on what must be done."

There was grumbling, but no real objection. Not from a witch, anyway.

"If you can just promise not to hurt one another, why didn't you do that before the meeting?" Owen asked the question that Rowe was thinking.

He got incredulous stares from more than a few witches. It was Julian who finally spoke up. "Conditions change quickly, and broken oaths extract a terrible price. We only make them in dire situations."

The situation certainly was dire.

The witches quickly circled together and chanted. Rowe couldn't quite understand the words they were saying. They all joined hands, and in a flash of blinding light, it was done.

He could feel a change in the air. And while

members of the rival covens still glared at one another, the threat of violence was quelled. For now.

His eye's met Vi's, and he nodded towards the forest.

It was time to hunt a monster.

CHAPTER
THIRTEEN

Vi wasn't going to think too hard about why her gaze had found Rowe's the second it was time to team up and go monster hunting. She knew every witch in her coven, and it wouldn't be bad to work with one of them.

Hell, even working with someone from Audra Palmer's coven might have been smart.

But no, she decided to work with the shifter who made her burn.

He said something to the rest of his team before coming to her side. And he waited until they were a bit away from everyone to speak. "Don't you want to warn them about the magic trap?"

That decision had been eating at her for the last two hours. Anyone could fall into it. It was a risk. But someone had put it there. Traps like that couldn't happen naturally. "If someone in Palmer's coven set it, I don't want to let on that I know about it," she finally said.

Rowe looked at her steadily for several seconds before speaking. "Or your coven."

She hadn't spoken those words, but the suspicion was there in the back of her mind just the same. "I know every single witch in my coven."

"And?" he prompted. "Are you saying they wouldn't do something like that?"

She wanted to agree. But she'd been gone for years. And some witches were always drawn to dark power, power that demanded blood. "Okay. I don't know who set it up, and I don't want to give it away. It's pretty far from where Ellie was hurt. Let's just hope no one gets caught in it."

He shrugged. "Okay."

"Okay? That's it?" She was angry, and she shouldn't have been. He was *agreeing* with her.

"You're the witch here. I'm trusting you on this, just like you trusted me in the woods." He stepped close until there was only a breath of space between them. Most of the other witches and shifters had already wandered off to make their hunting plans. No one was looking at them.

She wanted to kiss him.

She resisted.

Why did she have it so bad?

"Do you want to try and find Rosalie?" Rowe

asked, the subject change abrupt enough that her brain stuttered for a second.

"Rosalie? Why should we worry?" Rosalie was… somewhere safe. Vi was sure of that. For some reason. Her mind was a bit fuzzy on the why, but she knew she didn't have to go looking for her. Her coven leader didn't need to be bothered.

Rowe looked concerned. "Because no one has seen her in hours and there's a magical monster on the loose? Maybe we should just take a look around the camp to make sure she's okay. We can check in, then go on the hunt."

"That's a waste of time. Rosalie's…" Vi clamped her mouth shut. The words coming out felt *wrong*. And she didn't like her fuzzy head. "Yeah, let's take a look around the camp." Even though she was sure down to her soul that Rosalie was fine, she wanted to look.

What if someone was messing with her head?

Could the monster do that?

"I'm sure she's fine," Rowe said. Then he shook his head. "No. I'm not sure. Why would I think that?"

"Compulsion." It felt dirty to even suggest it.

"Are you saying that someone is messing with our brains?" He ran fingers through his hair as if that could somehow undo the spell.

"Maybe." She wasn't willing to commit yet. "Come on."

They scoured the campsite and finally circled around to Rosalie's cabin. She wasn't there. And the wrongness in Vi's head was only getting worse. Why wasn't Rosalie around?

She's fine, she thought, comfort seeping deep into her bones.

She's not *fine*, some other part of her yelled.

"Are you looking for Rosie?" Katrina Stevens, another member of Vi's coven, came up to them just as they walked away from Rosalie's cabin. "She's on the hunt. I saw her head into the woods with Delia a few minutes ago."

"Oh. Thanks." Vi had to take a minute to process the information, her brain still a bit sluggish.

"Everything alright?" Katrina asked.

"We're fine," Rowe assured her. "Are you hunting with someone?"

She nodded. "Darnell is packing some water and snacks before we go into the woods." She said her farewells and went to find Darnell.

"We worried for nothing," Vi said, but her words rang hollow.

"I guess." Rowe looked at Rosalie's cabin for a long time. Then he shook his head. "It's not like Katrina has a reason to lie."

"Right."

Still, it took them several minutes to walk away. But the further they went, the more assured Vi was that she'd worried for nothing.

But why hadn't Rosalie been there when Ellie was hurt?

The thought slid into and out of her mind so fast she barely caught the tail end of it. She stopped walking, trying to cling to it.

"Everything alright?" Rowe asked, stopping a few steps beyond her once he realized she wasn't moving.

She tried to catch the thought, but it was gone. "Yeah. Let's go."

Back in the forest, she put her whole mind to the task of searching for the monster that had attacked Ellie. Neither she nor Rowe spoke. But it wasn't necessary. They seemed to be in tune with one another, choosing paths and following trails without a need for words. With someone else, she had no doubt she'd be tripping over their feet or tearing her hair out from chit chat.

But not with Rowe.

She heard the roaring of a river in the distance and tried to recall the layout of the area. She should have spent more time looking at maps.

They didn't hear anyone else, but the forest was gigantic and more than capable of swallowing them whole. A grim thought, but true.

She stopped at the edge of a ravine and peered down. Could ravines go down that far? She saw the rushing water of the river but it was a long, *long* way down.

"Want to find a way around?" she asked Rowe. "Maybe if we head one way there will be a crossing point."

"If we can't get past it, do you think this magical monster could?" he asked logically.

She hoped the monster couldn't fly.

"I guess this is a dead end." She stepped away, but there was a crack, and she felt the dirt shift under her feet. She was falling.

Down.

And down.

And down.

Rowe didn't think, he just dived for Vi, reaching for any part of her as she disappeared from sight. He was too far away and moving too fast. He tumbled over the edge of the ravine right after her. For a moment, their eyes met in the air, and his certainty about their fate was reflected in her eyes.

They were going to die.

A wave of regret washed over him. He didn't want to die before he could claim his mate.

Then his body crashed against something hard and his vision went black, only for a second. They'd both landed on a ledge that jutted out from the ravine wall. It was as hard as stone, but packed with brown dirt with hints of greenery growing out of the ravine wall behind him. He was tempted to jump up and down a few times to test the strength of the ledge, but resisted.

They'd crashed into it and it had held. There was no reason to tempt fate.

The ledge was long enough that he and Vi could both lay on it with their sides against the ravine wall, and about five feet wide. There wasn't much room to maneuver, but the ledge had saved their lives, so he wasn't complaining.

Vi hadn't gotten up.

She'd landed first and hard, and Rowe was doing his best to give her a minute. He already could tell she wouldn't want to be crowded. She'd insist everything was fine, even if she was bleeding profusely. And all he wanted to do was tend to her.

The instinct was new. He'd never felt that way about a person before. But Vi was churning up feelings he'd never thought he'd feel.

Live, he willed her still form. *You have to live.*

He stared at her, afraid to touch. What if she'd broken something important? He had some first aid training, but nothing would fix a broken neck.

Her chest rose. Her breath came and went smoothly, with no rattle that might indicate broken ribs.

He knelt at her side, one foot hanging off the ledge. He picked up her hand and weaved their fingers together once he was satisfied they weren't broken. A sense of rightness washed over him at the connection. He needed to be touching her.

Her eyes opened and she glared at him.

He smiled.

His witch was back.

She sucked in a deep breath and winced. Rowe leaned even closer, but she was already sitting up and waving him off. "I'm fine, I'm fine."

"Careful, you could have internal bleeding." At this point he was more using knowledge gleaned from television medical procedurals than Army training. Where was a hot TV doctor when you needed her?

"I don't have internal bleeding," Vi snapped. "Back up or you're going to have *external* bleeding. Jeez, I need space to breathe."

He couldn't resist. He kissed her forehead, so relieved she was alive and almost well. Then he scurried back before she could push him off the ledge.

"We're not dead," Vi said after a minute. They were sitting close together, legs brushing. She could have moved away.

Rowe didn't have it in him to put any distance between them. Despite Vi's grouchiness, the same seemed to be true for her. "We are not dead," he agreed.

She leaned forward and looked over the ledge, and then shot back until she was pressed up against the ravine wall. "That was a mistake. Shit, we are lucky."

"Afraid of heights?" It was half taunt, half

concern. His heart might have been demanding he claim her, but he was still himself.

"This isn't heights. This is suicide." She looked up to where they'd fallen from. "And that is Mount Everest."

Rowe gave it a look. "It's just a few feet," or twenty. Almost straight up, but with a lot of handholds. At least they hadn't fallen down a sheer cliff. "You up for a climb?"

"You're fucking crazy." She got to her feet and faced the ravine wall, reaching her hands as high as they could go.

"What are you doing?" he asked. He liked the way Vi's body looked all stretched out like that, but now was not the time to be focusing on her body. But once they were safe, all bets were off.

Rowe's cock liked that.

Fuck. He needed to focus.

Vi squinted as she looked at the top of the ravine. "I'm trying to figure out how far it is to get up there. Three body lengths? Four?" She waved her hands and wiggled her fingers as if that might help.

"It's about twenty feet." He didn't need to reach his arms up or contort into any position to figure that out.

She glared at him. And there had to be something scrambled in his brain, because he only liked her more. "So you can just tell? Some special shifter sense?"

"Or a trick I learned in the Army." He grinned at her. "Come on. This is nothing. You can do it." They hadn't fallen *that* far.

Vi bent her arm like she was showing off a bicep and smacked her muscles. "Do I look like the kind of person with the upper body strength for a twenty-foot free climb?"

He forced himself not to stare at any part of her body. No distractions. And if he'd learned one thing about his… Vi in the past hours, it was that she rose to a challenge. "Not with that attitude." He wasn't going to make any more statements about her body, no matter how much he wanted it.

And some people said he wasn't a smart man.

"I can't do it." Vi sagged, her arms falling to her sides. She sounded defeated.

"You're not even willing to try?" He was going to get her off this ledge. Somehow. "I can boost you at least half of the way up. And depending on the hand-holds, I might even be able to push you further. We can do this together."

Vi eyed the ravine wall again, her jaw set. "I know my limits."

"Try," he insisted. He was going to push her until she climbed just to spite him.

She made a sound of frustration but stepped close to him, one finger poking at his chest. "Fine. But when I die because I fell and broke my neck, I am going to hunt you for the rest of your existence. Got it?"

"Got it." But she wasn't going to die. Not on his watch.

He boosted her up, and she managed to find a handhold. Her feet dangled until she could find a foothold.

"Don't rely on your arms," he told her, wincing in sympathy as she struggled. He wanted to help, but this was something she had to do herself. "Your legs are where your strength is at. Use them. Find a foothold and move to it. Then move your arms. You can do this."

He thought it was going to work. He thought she was going to do it. He even had his hands on the ravine wall ready to climb up after her. But after making it two more feet up the wall, Vi lost her footing and fell.

Rowe caught her.

She pushed away from him and let out a furious shriek as she slapped her hand against the ravine wall before pulling it back and shaking it to ward off the pain.

"Told you." She sank down and pulled her legs in close, wrapping her arms around her knees. "You can make the climb. You should go and find help." She reached into her pocket and pulled out her cell phone. She checked the screen and then flashed it at him. "I don't have any reception. This area has terrible service. Check yours."

That was probably something they should have done first, but his brain was still a bit wobbly from nearly dying. He checked his phone and found that he also didn't have service. "I won't leave you here." Wolf and man were in agreement. Vi needed to be protected.

"You may not have another choice," she countered.

To hell with that. There was always another choice. "Can't you do magic or something? I don't know, fly up to the edge of the ravine? Or use your powers to make a magic phone call?"

She tilted her head to the side and looked at him like he had grown extra limbs. "You really don't understand magic, do you?"

He grinned back at her. She was starting to sound more like the Vi he knew. He wouldn't let her get dispirited.

She rolled her eyes. "I could *maybe* send up a magical flare. But if the monster is anywhere nearby, that's gonna call him to us. I don't exactly want to fight him if he comes down here."

Good point. He slid down to sit beside her, and his arm went around her shoulders as if it was meant to be there. He tugged her close.

"Someone will find us," he said with unearned

confidence. "There are twenty people out there who will notice we're missing. We just have to be patient."

"It's stupid for both of us to wait here," she said. "You should go." But she laid her head against his shoulder.

She knew he wasn't going anywhere.

Now they just had to hope that one of the witches or shifters found them before the monster lurking in the woods did.

Vi knew she should be arguing for Rowe to leave. They'd been cuddled up on the ledge for nearly half an hour with no sign of anyone coming to find them. Of course, no one would realize they were missing for hours. If they were lucky, they *might* be found by morning.

If they were found at all.

Her stupid shifter wasn't budging, even though he was in the best position to go get help. And she hated that she was a little grateful he refused to leave. She wasn't exactly afraid of heights, but she didn't trust the ledge they were perched on, and she'd already felt the unforgiving grip of gravity once today.

She didn't want to fall even further.

And Rowe was so warm.

The day hadn't been that chilly when they went

out into the woods, and she did have a light jacket on. But the ravine seemed to suck up wind and batter them with it. It felt ten degrees colder here than it had higher up.

She was fooling herself if she believed that was the only reason she was cuddled up to Rowe. But he wasn't pulling away or asking for anything. She could just soak up this connection for as long as it lasted.

She really hoped it didn't last the rest of their lives. Not if that meant freezing to death and never being found.

"Have you been with Rosalie's coven long?" Rowe asked after a while. He picked up her hand and traced the creases of her palm.

It felt good, intimate. Right. But Vi refused to examine that too closely. "Since I was a kid. I left for a few years, and I just returned after I left Mercy's— Em's—tour." It was strange to consider that one of the biggest rock stars on the planet was sort of her friend. "Is everything going alright with her?"

Rowe shifted his position, and she found herself pressed even closer to him. "Yeah, all's good. I'm pretty sure Andre is her personal bodyguard for life now. It sucks a bit. I liked working with him."

"He's still a part of your pack, isn't he?" Rowe and his people were the strangest shifters she'd ever met. They were brimming with power in a way that Nora West and her people weren't, but they were so ignorant of themselves they might as well have been human.

"I don't know, no one else has left before." He was contemplative. "I'm not sure any of us understands how our… pack… functions."

"Still feels weird?" She couldn't imagine what it would be like to be thrust into the magical world the way they had all been. She'd been born a witch. Magic was her life.

"You know the story?"

She recalled hearing it from Andre. "Evil magic doers in Germany, a kidnapping of a bunch of American soldiers, and you all became shifters months later? Am I missing anything?" It sounded fake, but she could shoot energy bolts out of her hands, so who was she to judge?

"That's about it. Why did you leave?"

"Leave?" She flipped their hands. It was her turn to explore him.

"The coven."

Her heart stuttered, but it didn't break. The searing pain that had nearly broken her had dissipated over the years.

And Noah had never made her feel like she did with Rowe.

She tried to keep her tone light, both to protect her heart and because she was pretty sure her shifter wouldn't like hearing about her first love and heartbreak. "My ex and I were together for years. Ever since high school. Then, a couple years ago, every-thing seemed to go wrong. It's screwed up. I can't even remember why we fought or what about. He said I lied to him? But I never did, at least not inten-tionally. He was playing mind games. He broke it off, and I left. I couldn't stand to see him all the time."

Rowe was quiet, dangerously so, but he didn't pull away from her. "And he's still part of the coven?" Something feral echoed in his words.

"You can't attack my ex-boyfriend. He's not a terrible person. We just didn't work out." It had taken her years to realize that, but now she did. Now it was okay.

"He's a fool."

"Well, duh." His serious tone made her smile. And she needed to throw something back at him before she did something stupid. Like throw *herself* at him. "Why were you in jail?"

"I wasn't *in jail*," he sputtered. "I was in the lobby of a police station. Completely different."

"So you didn't spend the night in a cell?" She nudged him with her shoulder, daring him to lie.

"I wasn't booked. It won't be on my record."

"You seem to know a lot about the process. Not your first arrest?" How could she even be joking about this? She wasn't supposed to be attracted to guys who were too familiar with the wrong side of the criminal justice system.

At least Rowe's mood didn't sour at the questions. "I got in a fight at a bar."

"Oh, a bar fight! Great!" What was fate doing to her? Was *this* really the man for her?

"A bouncer at the bar was hassling his ex. I tried to stop it. Things… escalated." He scowled.

"You're a wolf. You could snap most humans in half." Sure, he didn't know much about being a shifter, but Vi couldn't let him get away with harming humans. They had a responsibility to people, and to keeping the secret of the supernatural world.

His laugh was harsh. "Matty is not most humans. He's twice my size and loves to fight. Besides, I know how to pull my punches. I wasn't going to let him hurt that woman."

Vi couldn't hold back anymore. She slid her hand up to cup Rowe's neck and kissed him with everything she had. Their earlier kiss had been a thing of desperation, an affirmation that they were alive and that the magic hadn't beaten them.

This was a thing of want.

An admission.

She couldn't fight this thing between them, and she didn't want to. Why should she? Her body cried out for his. Her heart knew exactly who he was.

Fighting fate was a fool's errand. And Vi was no fool.

Rowe let her keep control of the kiss, her tongue

teasing his, her lips nipping when he wasn't close enough. She needed him with her. If she wasn't afraid of rolling off the ledge, she'd be stripping him of his clothing right that second.

Instead, she got to savor the kiss. They couldn't do much more, not with the logistics of their position.

But she could kiss him for hours.

Maybe the ledge was a blessing in disguise.

Then Rowe swept her up and laid her down, pressing her to the ground with the strength of his body and claiming her mouth like he owned her. It was a battering ram of seduction and almost too forceful. But here in this secret place where only the two of them existed, she gave into it.

She reveled in it.

She had a hard time giving up control. She knew who she was, she knew what she wanted, and she wasn't any man's plaything.

But Rowe's insistent kisses claimed her in a way she'd always secretly wanted to be claimed. They marked her as his.

And she happily surrendered to it.

She forgot herself in the kiss, let the sensation wash over her, and moved by instinct, thrusting her hips up. She wanted on top of Rowe, wanted to leave marks of her own.

He moved.

And her passion almost sent him to his doom.

He was ripped away from her and gave a startled cry. They'd been tangling close to the edge, closer than she realized.

Half his body dangled off the side, and he was frozen. She didn't think; instead, she grabbed on and yanked him back, imbuing her strength with magic in a way she wasn't certain would work.

But she needed it to work.

Rowe scrambled to safety, his breathing labored and his lips swollen from their kiss.

Then he smiled. "I think I saw a way down."

CHAPTER
SIXTEEN

Vi yelled at Rowe as he carefully lowered himself over the ledge to get a better look at the path he'd half seen when he nearly tumbled to his doom. Her hand was on his wrist, a reminder that if he fell, she was coming with him.

So he wouldn't fall.

He couldn't see very well while he was hanging from his hands, so he pulled himself up over the ledge and rolled around to let his upper body hang off.

"Anchor my legs," he told Vi.

'You'll be lucky if I don't push you off," she muttered, but she grabbed onto his ankles.

Rowe's abs worked hard to keep him suspended there, but he saw what he needed to see. The river *was* a long way down, but there was a trail less than ten feet under their ledge, and it appeared to wend its way back up to the top of the ravine. The jump would be a little tricky, but gravity would do the hard work.

He sat back up on the ledge and smiled at Vi. "Come on, let's get out of here."

Her eyes went wide, and she shook her head. "Didn't you see that drop?"

"There's a trail. Come look." He waved her over to the edge of the ledge.

She moved cautiously, and he wasn't sure if it was distrust of the ground beneath them or him that had her looking like that. She blew out a breath. "If we miss the landing, we're dead."

"We're not going to miss the landing. Are you wearing a belt?"

The sudden question seemed to make her thoughts stutter. "What?"

"A belt?" Rowe reached for his own and undid it. "Do you have one?"

"Yes. Why?"

"Give it to me." He held out his hand. "Trust me, I have an idea."

She pulled off her belt, a thick leather strap that was sure to hold up, and handed it to him. "I shouldn't trust you."

"But you do." He knew it deep in his bones.

"But I do." She didn't sound happy about it.

Rowe linked their two belts together. They weren't quite six feet long, but he hoped they would do the job. "You're going to hold onto the belt and I'll lower you," he said. "Then you can swing over and let go when you're in the right spot. Sound good?"

Vi fingered the edge of the leather. "Sounds suicidal. How are you supposed to get down?"

"I'm going to jump. I've got this." And he was pretty sure he did. At least seventy percent sure. Seventy-three percent sure.

She stared at the belt for a long time before swiftly leaning forward and capturing his lips in a searing kiss. "Don't die."

Seventy-seven percent sure, now. "I won't," he promised.

Rowe didn't let himself think of the possibility of failure. He wasn't going to hurt Vi, and she was going to make it down easily. There was no other option. She started to swing, and his heart leapt into his throat when she let go of the belts, her weight suddenly gone from his hands.

Then he heard a thud as she landed on the trail below them.

"I'm okay!" she assured him. "But be careful, it's kind of narrow. You might want to try and climb back up. I can meet you there."

That would be the sane thing to do.

Rowe wasn't sane when it came to Vi.

He didn't let himself think too hard as he swung down and let go of the edge, arcing in the air until his feet met the ground right beside her.

Her mouth dropped open, and he could feel the threat of magic crackle in the air. "You—"

He grinned. "Piece of cake."

She let up a burst of sparks, as if she had to let the magic go *somewhere*. "I'm going to murder you."

"You'll miss me when I'm gone." He stepped even closer to her. He wanted to kiss her, but he still had some of his faculties left. She really might kill him if he got too close.

"Let's try it and see." But instead of pushing him back, she fisted her hands in the fabric of his shirt and held onto him.

He wrapped his arms around her and felt muscles he hadn't known were tense relax. "We're okay. We're going to make it."

They stood like that for several minutes. Rowe could have stood there forever. But in the distance, the sun was starting to sink, and the shadows were growing long. He didn't want to navigate the trail back up to the forest at night.

They separated, and Vi didn't argue when Rowe led the way.

For all the drama of their fall, the path back up was clear and easy to follow. It took them less than ten minutes to make it all the way back up, and it was like they'd never fallen.

"We should probably head back to camp," Vi suggested. "I'm not sure it's a smart idea to hunt a monster by moonlight."

Rowe agreed. "Maybe another team had better luck." With weak cell reception, it wasn't like a notification would have gone out.

They headed in the direction of the camp, but they'd wandered a long way before their fall. It was getting harder and harder to see, even with Rowe's slightly enhanced shifter vision.

"Wait." Vi put her hand on his shoulder to stop him. "I think I sense magic."

"Another witch?" There were more than a dozen in these woods.

She thought for a moment. "It's familiar but... not. I swear I should recognize it, but there's something wrong with the magic."

"The monster?" Of course they'd run into the beast when they were tired and losing the light. Rowe wondered if he was cursed. Maybe that would explain today's luck.

But it couldn't all be bad when he still had the taste of Vi on his lips.

Vi took the lead, her hands glowing with magic. Rowe stuck close behind. His fingers itched for a gun, but he didn't carry one. And he wasn't sure a gun would do much against a magical monster.

Branches snapped somewhere in front of them, and Vi froze. She sent a soft wave of magic out, and Rowe was mesmerized as the glow illuminated the woods for a moment, then it was gone.

Until an animal roared.

His wolf strained under his skin, demanding that he shift and protect his mate, but Rowe held his ground for now. It would take crucial seconds to shift, and both he and Vi would be defenseless.

Claws strained and burst through his skin. He hissed in pain, but thanked his wolf for the weapon, even if he didn't fully understand how it was possible.

A huge black figure lumbered toward them. Rowe was ready to strike, but Vi sent out a violent burst of magic that sent the monster stumbling back.

"Run," Vi commanded. She yanked on his arm and pulled him back. "That only stunned it."

They ran.

The forest blurred around them, but after only a little while, they slowed down. The monster wasn't following.

"It was a black bear," Vi panted out, bent over and trying to regain her breath. "Black bears don't act like that. And they certainly shouldn't be dripping with magic."

Rowe turned it over in his head as they walked. She was right, black bears generally didn't attack people. And that bear had been acting more like a grizzly. A grizzly on steroids.

What was making it do that?

The sun had fully set by the time they made it back to camp, and lights were on in a few of the tiny houses. No one was waiting outside.

He and Vi walked down the small street and stopped in front of his house. Hers was a bit further on.

"Want to come in?" he asked. He didn't care how small the house was anymore. It just meant he could be closer to Vi. "I can make us some coffee." He thought he'd seen a coffee machine.

"I don't want coffee."

"Want to come in anyway?" he asked. The thing between them was a madness he didn't want to end.

Vi grabbed his hand and smiled. "Yeah. I think I do."

CHAPTER
SEVENTEEN

Vi didn't know what she expected from Rowe's cabin. She was willing to guess his apartment back in the city was a bit messy. But he'd only had the cabin for a few hours, and most of those hours had been spent in the forest.

It looked just like hers, tiny and neat.

The bed was already set up and it took up almost all of the room. Good. At least the universe was doing one thing right today.

She didn't rush into bed with people. She'd had more than one date make assumptions about her based on the fun colors in her hair and her leather jackets, but they were idiots. She didn't sleep with every guy she dated. They had to make it worth her while.

And Rowe?

She wouldn't have believed it on the day they

met, even if she had the gift of prophecy. But they'd come a long way in a short time, and she was determined to have him.

While he was turned away, she set her shoes beside the door and pulled off her shirt. When he turned back, he dropped his phone.

She hoped the screen didn't crack. But if it did, there would be a grim satisfaction in knowing she'd left that mark on his life.

"Take your clothes off," she commanded. She stepped close—not that it was possible to put any distance between them in the cabin—and pushed him back towards the bed. He only had to take half a step before he ran into it.

Rowe's eyes flashed golden for a second, and it was like she was looking right at his wolf. That was impossible. Shifters couldn't show their animal traits in human form.

And yet she was looking at Rowe with her own two eyes.

He took his shirt off and tossed it somewhere behind her. She felt like a magnet drawn to his iron hard abs, and he hissed out a breath when her fingers caressed him. He was hot to the touch, so warm she feared he'd burn her up.

But what a way to go.

She traced her hands over his exposed skin. If she thought too hard, she'd remember how close they'd come to not making it back here. They could have still been hanging on that ledge right now, hoping for a rescue she doubted would ever come.

But they were alive. And together.

He kissed her.

His fingers tangled in her hair and he cradled her head, holding her close and controlling her in a way she would have fought if he was any other man. But this wasn't any other man, this was Rowe, her... wolf.

She still couldn't dwell on the other word, even as his kiss overwhelmed her senses and made her forget all her troubles.

Who cared about a monster when a beast was about to take her to bed?

He undid her bra with the kind of ease that might have led to teasing if she was in the mood for anything but skin on skin. This man knew his way around a woman's body. But she wasn't about to get caught up in petty jealousy.

He was hers, and she wasn't letting him go.

She hitched her legs up around his waist and he supported her, turning and setting her on the bed, his body coming over hers, a welcome weight that made her moan. His scent enveloped her, the imprint of the woods still on him entwined with raw masculinity that made her thighs clench.

She needed all of him, but she didn't want to let him go. She couldn't. Not when they could finally celebrate that they were alive.

The things this man made her feel weren't something she knew how to handle or resist. He was temptation incarnate, designed specifically to make her yearn. And yearn she did. Feelings she wasn't ready to face threatened to bubble up, her heart, mind, and body all in accord.

Rowe, this man, this shifter—he was *hers*.

He kissed down her body, his lips finding a nipple and making her arch up into him as his tongue did wicked things to her. She might have been the witch, but she was under his spell.

And it wasn't just his tongue. His hand cupped her other breast, his fingers teasing her until she moaned. This was dark magic. Dark, sensual sorcery that was going to bind her up and never let her walk away.

Rowe wasn't rushed. Vi wanted to move him on, to race him to the aching crescendo that would take them both to the heights of pleasure before letting them go in a wave of release. But her wolf wanted to savor her.

She didn't know that patience could drive a woman crazy.

Her fingers tangled in the sheets beside her. She needed to hold onto something, or she feared she would come undone.

She wanted more. She wanted everything.

And she wanted to torture him with pleasure.

Vi sent a jolt of power at Rowe, little more than a

static shock, but enough to get his attention. His pupils were wide and his lips wet when he looked up at her. "No?" he asked.

She pushed him back until she was on top of him and then slid her way down his body. "My turn."

He groaned, and sat back as she opened the fly of his jeans and freed his aching cock from the confines of his pants. He was leaking at the tip, swollen and on the edge of coming.

Vi leaned down and licked his cock head, luxuriating in the taste of him and the way he gasped out her name. But she wasn't ready to give him her whole mouth, not quite yet. She wrapped her palm around him and stroked, watching as his jaw tightened and his eyes closed in pleasure.

Oh, yeah. He liked this.

"Tighter," he gritted out, thrusting into her grip.

Vi tightened her grip. And she moved faster too. She wanted to watch him fall apart. Her body was on fire, empty and aching and wanting more. But first she wanted to witness this intimate act.

"I can't hold on," he warned her. His muscles bunched up as if he was holding back a thousand-ton weight.

"Don't," she said, leaning closer and kissing his neck. "I want to see."

That was all it took. He came with a roar, his whole body clenching as he shot in her hand.

He took a second to get his bearings, and there

was something wolfish in his gaze as he tackled her to the bed, the remnants of his release smearing between them.

"I need to taste you." Something primal echoed in his voice, and Vi shivered under him. There was no resisting this, and she didn't want to.

She wanted whatever Rowe planned to do to her.

He got her pants off of her in a feat of coordination she wasn't sure she could muster if she was riding the high of orgasm.

Then he spread her legs and feasted.

Vi moaned loudly. She didn't care about the acute senses of anyone outside of this little house. All that mattered was the man between her thighs and the pleasure he brought her.

If she'd thought it was good when he worshiped her breasts, she was in another world now. Her wolf seemed to tap into her mind, reading her body and ratcheting up the pleasure before she even thought to ask. She writhed against him, one hand digging into his hair and holding him tight to her.

Not that he was leaving.

His tongue laved against her and swirled at her most sensitive point. She thought she would go mad with the onslaught of pleasure.

Then he splayed her open with his fingers and it got even better.

She couldn't take it much longer. Her heart pounded so fast she would have worried it was about to explode, if she was capable of thinking of anything but the ecstasy Rowe gave her in that moment.

Release slammed into her and Vi gave herself over to it, her body rippling and her mouth gasping, calling out his name and begging him for more.

Eventually, her body calmed down. Rowe kissed her inner thighs before crawling up the bed to cuddle her close. It wasn't that late, but the excitement of the day and pleasure of the night had wrung her out until she could barely keep her eyes open.

And as her mate wrapped his arm around her, she was helpless to resist the comfort of sleep.

But at the edge of her mind, she remembered there was a monster out there, and they were going to have to face it.

CHAPTER
EIGHTEEN

Rowe was fine with Vi going back to her cabin after a loud noise woke them both up. Completely, totally fine. It was a hookup. They were happy they were alive. It definitely didn't feel like he'd bared his soul and had been left flayed open for her to do whatever she pleased.

He scowled.

This was bad. Worse than bad.

No woman had ever burrowed under his skin like this. Even now he wanted to follow her and hold her through the night. She didn't want to sleep in his cabin? Fine. They could both sleep in hers.

But he didn't head her way. He wasn't that desperate.

Not yet.

The walls of the tiny house were closing in on him. He needed air. He threw on a pair of sweats and opened the door, dragging in deep breaths of the fresh, green night breeze. New York never smelled like this. It was almost tempting.

Then he remembered just how far away they were from the nearest… anything. He'd suffer the city stench if it meant he didn't have to drive an hour for groceries.

He sank down onto the stairs in front of his cabin and rested his head in his hands. He felt like he was going crazy. His inner wolf grumbled at him, telling him that he was crazy for letting Vi go. His wolf insisted that she was his mate and he needed to stop fighting it.

He'd seen how quickly Owen had fallen to his own mate. How long had it taken? Three days? Four? And did Rowe have him beat? Sure, he and Vi had met earlier in the week, but in some ways, this was their first real day together.

It wasn't a fucking contest.

And then there was Andre. Had his mind been so scrambled by the urge to claim his mate?

Claim? What the hell did that even mean?

He wanted Vi at his side. He wanted everyone to know that Vi was his. And he wanted to be hers. Hell, he was almost tempted to go buy a ring, so he knew he was nuts. He'd vowed to himself that he'd never be one of those soldiers who married a woman after a whirlwind weekend.

At least he wasn't a soldier anymore.

Where *was* she? The simple answer was that she was back in her cabin, sleeping peacefully and not caring a bit about him. Energy thrummed in Rowe's veins, and it took all of his self-control to stay in place.

He wasn't a sad puppy dog. He wasn't going to chase after her.

He stood up and paced. And then he decided his ridiculously small house was finally good for something. He marched around it, not bothering to count the laps. On any other night, he might have gone for a long walk in the woods, but he wasn't a fool. There was a monster out there, and Rowe wasn't going to make himself a target.

But he was spoiling for a fight.

"Fuck!" He tripped on nothing and glared at the ground. That woman had him so messed up that he couldn't even focus on walking, something he'd been more than competent at for over thirty years.

"You okay there, buddy?" Owen was sitting on the front step of Rowe's cabin and watching him with unhidden delight.

Rowe glared. He didn't know how anyone put up with the man's annoyingly good moods. He was surprised Owen's mate hadn't stabbed him yet. "Shouldn't you be in your cabin? It's late."

Owen snorted. "It's not even ten o'clock."

Was that true? This had been one of the longest

days of Rowe's life, if he didn't count the day he'd been kidnapped and transformed into a werewolf.

"I just did a sweep of the camp," Owen continued in his irrepressibly cheery tone. "No monsters."

"There's a relief." Rowe nudged Owen to the side and sat next to him on the step. "You catch sight of it in the woods earlier?"

"No." That took a bit of his cheer away.

Good.

"We did." Rowe should have reported it to Gibson the moment he got back. Instead, he'd been so focused on Vi that he'd put the job aside.

"Gibson's going to want to know. What did you see?" Owen didn't sound judgmental, but Rowe was sure there'd be a reaming out by the time he talked to his boss.

"It's a black bear. A mean one." He could see its claws in his head, and all he could imagine was those claws digging into Vi and ripping her to shreds.

"We're all freaked out because of a bear in the woods? The woods where bears normally live?"

"This wasn't a normal bear." Rowe hadn't ever seen a bear in the woods before, but he was absolutely sure of that.

Owen blew out a breath. "First it's ghost wolves, now it's abnormal bears. What's next? Flying goats?"

"Goats can jump pretty high already." Rowe had seen more than one internet video to prove it.

"Let's save the flying goats for Vega and Jackson, they can deal with it." Then Owen grinned at him. "So what's the deal with the witch? Want to talk about it?"

He almost did. His hopes and his fears bubbled to the surface, and for a crazy moment, Rowe almost said something. Owen was the first of their weird little pack to find his mate. He and his doctor were figuring things out as they went along. And if there was anyone who would understand what Rowe thought he was feeling, it was Owen.

But was Vi really his mate?

What if Owen said he was wrong?

He wasn't about to let the guy be the final authority on his own feelings, but Owen was the closest thing to an expert that Rowe could ask.

And he didn't want to know. Not if it meant that Vi wasn't…

He was fucking crazy.

"Go finish your sweep," Rowe told him with a shove. "This isn't a sleepover. We're not staying up all night to talk about our crushes."

"A crush?" Owen's eyes widened in delight. "This is more serious than I thought."

"Fuck off." He wasn't going to smile. That would only encourage Owen.

The chipper werewolf wandered off, still laughing, and Rowe was once again alone. He looked up and spied the half moon overhead and wondered if it could give him guidance.

But if werewolves were supposed to have some sort of connection to the moon, Rowe didn't know how to trigger it. And he went back into his cabin with no answers and a heaviness in his heart.

CHAPTER
NINETEEN

Something nagged at Vi. And it wasn't just the urge to go back to Rowe's cabin and snuggle up with him for the rest of the night. Or forever. *That* instinct was almost too strong to ignore. But she had to. For her own sanity.

If she got hooked on Rowe, he could break her heart. A guy like that wasn't made for forever.

He's your mate, a frustrated voice whispered in her mind.

But she wasn't sure. She'd never thought she'd end up mated to a shifter, but she knew the signs. And some of them were sparking hot between her and Rowe.

Immediate, undeniable attraction.

Possessiveness.

Certainty in her soul that he belonged to her.

He could still walk away. So could she, for that

matter. They weren't prisoners of fate. It would hurt. They'd both be tearing their hearts out to do it, but she'd heard of potential mates who threw the bond away.

Would Rowe do that if he knew it was an option?

Should she?

She made it to her cabin and had her hand on the door, but she couldn't go inside. That something was still nagging her.

Why had Rosalie called this meeting?

What was going on in the woods?

She recalled her certainty earlier in the day that everything had been fine with her coven leader, and now it rang hollow in her head. They'd been in the midst of a crisis and Rosalie was nowhere to be found.

Why hadn't Vi cared?

Was Rosalie—

The thought ran into a brick wall in her head.

Vi turned around and eyed the central meeting hall. Rosalie had been setting things up there earlier in the day, so maybe she could find some answers there. Or she could find her coven leader and ask some questions.

What was Rosalie's problem with Audra Palmer and her coven? Did she really think the other woman was responsible for the violence against local witches?

Vi hadn't spent much time with Palmer, but the

woman didn't seem deranged or violent. Then again, monsters were very good at hiding.

The binding agreement to do no harm was still in place, so she wasn't too concerned about walking around. No one from the other coven would hurt her tonight.

And Rowe would come running if she called for him.

She tried to ignore that certainty. She wasn't about to start depending on the wolf just because they'd shared orgasms. They needed to have a discussion, but not tonight. She knew he and his pack were nearly completely ignorant about… everything. So it was going to be her job to teach him.

And she'd have a duty to make sure he understood *all* of his options.

Magic burbled under her skin, and she took deep breaths to settle it. She didn't need to borrow trouble from tomorrow when there was plenty more to find tonight.

She didn't see anyone walking around the cabins, but she did her best to keep to the shadows, just in case. She didn't want questions about why she was out and about. Not that she was doing anything wrong. There wasn't a curfew.

There were no lights on in the recreation building, but Vi's eyes were already adjusted to the dark outside. Large windows let in moonlight, and she could see well enough.

Not that there was much *to* see.

A large table ran the length of the room, with enough chairs for a few dozen people. They were supposed to all share a meal tomorrow, and this would be the spot. Earlier, Rosalie had been using the table and had covered it in folders, but all the papers were gone.

Not exactly surprising. Rosalie was a neat person, and with a rival coven crawling over every inch of the camp, she wouldn't risk leaving out anything important.

She looked around a bit more, just in case there was something to find, but the room was spotless. Vi yawned. What time was it? Whenever it was, the day's excitement was starting to weigh heavy on her.

She wanted to go to bed and curl up beside Rowe.

She groaned. That wasn't what she was going to do. She was going back to her *own* cabin and her *own* lonely bed. She didn't need some giant shifter hogging all the covers.

With a final look to make sure everything was in place, Vi left the building. Despite the monster lurking out in the woods, there was a certain peacefulness to the camp that made her breathe easier. It was nice to be out of the city for a moment.

Leaves crunched to her right.

Vi jerked her head, but didn't see anything. She stopped moving and barely breathed. And *there*, more sound. Faint, but there.

She crept closer. It wasn't the monster. No monster would be so quiet. But someone was being sneaky.

Two someones, actually.

She recognized the woman with the blonde braid as Nora, the other coven's head shapeshifter. The man with her was a witch from the other coven. Julian something. He'd been the one to prepare the healing spell for the wounded witch.

What were they doing out so late?

They stood close and spoke too quietly for Vi to hear. She tried to get closer, but she didn't want to risk them seeing her.

Julian put his hand on Nora's forearm and tugged her closer. The shifter went.

Interesting.

Then Vi stepped on some of the same leaves that had given them away, and they both jerked their heads towards her.

"What are you doing out?" Nora asked, putting space between her and Julian and stepping in front of him in case Vi attacked.

"I could ask the same of you." Vi didn't call on her magic. She didn't want to start a fight.

Nora tilted her head up and breathed deep. Then she grinned, but it was all malice. "Couldn't resist taking a wolf to bed?"

"You seem to like witches yourself." She wasn't going to be ashamed of what she and Rowe had done. She was an adult. And even if her mind was a bit scattered about what it all meant, it had been fun.

Julian sneered as he stepped from behind Nora. "Come to lure us into another trap?"

"A trap?" Was he talking about the magic tree? Had someone else found it? Vi should not have kept it secret. But this scowling witch wasn't going to be the first person she told.

Her own coven leader needed to know first.

"I don't know what game you're playing, but you won't win." Julian stalked off before she could ask any questions.

Nora went in the other direction.

Vi stayed where she was. She wasn't sure what was going on, but she wasn't going to waste time following the shifter or the witch.

She explored around the recreation center for a little bit, looking for any kind of clue. Her eyes didn't see anything.

But her eyes weren't her only sense.

Vi summoned a flicker of magic. She didn't want to use a lot, didn't want to summon another witch or alert anyone to what she was doing. She poured all of her intent into that spark, hoping it could show her something.

Then she let the magic free and followed it. If there was anything in range, she would find it.

At first the magic seemed to freeze in the air, a

sign there was nothing to discover. And then it jerked towards the woods.

Vi wanted to call it back. She wasn't suicidal. Nothing except the most dire circumstances would send her into those woods alone at night.

The magic stopped before it hit the trees and sank down to the ground, glowing for a second before it extinguished.

At first, Vi thought she had reached the edge of the range the flicker could explore. Then she looked where it had fallen.

Something small and white caught her eye.

It was a molar. But it didn't look human. And it was absolutely dripping with dark magic.

Vi didn't touch it. She didn't want to be contaminated with whatever was swirling around in the bone.

She slipped off her shoe and stripped off her sock. Then she carefully picked the molar up with the sock. She'd do more tests later.

She put her bare foot back into her shoe and held the sock tightly in her hand.

She had her clue. Now she just had to figure out what it meant.

CHAPTER
TWENTY

Rowe's head was pounding, and the grit in his eyes was driving him crazy. He'd barely slept. His time in the Army meant that he could sack out just about anywhere.

But he wasn't in the Army anymore, and his brain was beginning to catch up to that fact.

He wanted to curse, but he hadn't even had his coffee yet. The stupid tiny house's stupid tiny coffee maker was broken. There was a good chance that he'd demolish that fancy shed before this job was over. Right now, the only thing keeping him from doing it was that it was probably stupidly expensive.

He was sure that if Vi had slept in bed beside him his sleep would have gone on just fine. His wolf rumbled under his skin. Yeah, the wolf agreed too. He shouldn't have let Vi leave.

And how could he make her stay? Handcuffs?

His cock twitched at the idea. But he had a feeling that if either of them was getting tied up, it was him. Vi wasn't the kind to give up control easily. And she'd make it good for him.

He needed to find her. They needed to talk. Or fuck. Preferably both.

Though the instinct beat at him hard to go find his… Vi, he fought back against it. He was here to do a job. And he'd been failing.

Gibson might forgive him for not reporting in last night. But it meant that Rowe had to report right now.

He made a quick detour away from Vi's cabin. Gibson had just stepped out of the shower when Rowe knocked on his door. The major's hair was wet, and he'd hastily pulled on a shirt. It clung to his still damp skin.

He gave Rowe an unimpressed look but invited him into the cabin.

Why was the major's cabin bigger than his? *Was* it actually bigger? Or was the major's tendency to keep things antiseptically neat somehow making the place feel even bigger?

Rowe wasn't going to question it. Gibson was pissed at him enough, he didn't need remarks about any perceived sloppiness.

The sooner this job was over, the sooner he could go home. More importantly, he could figure out what was going on between himself and Vi.

"Owen said he talked to you last night," Gibson told him. He leaned against the small counter and picked up a coffee mug with steam wafting off of it. Of course *he* had a functioning coffee maker. "He said that you would report in the morning."

Rowe needed to give Owen a fruit basket or something. The guy had just saved his ass. And he wasn't about to waste the opportunity. He stood up a little straighter. "Right. I wanted to let you know what Vi and I saw yesterday in the forest."

Gibson nodded for him to continue and sipped his coffee.

Rowe told him everything: walking through the forest, getting stuck on the ledge, encountering the black bear monster. He even mentioned the magic tree again, just to make sure that Gibson remembered.

When he was done talking, Gibson had a dark look on his face.

"You withheld information from the team." He set his mug down with a *clink*. "What the hell were you thinking?"

Rowe wished he knew. Every excuse that came to mind would get him fired on the spot. Maybe he deserved to be fired. He kept his mouth shut. It was the best he could do.

"Are you keeping anything else from me?" Gibson's voice was dangerously neutral.

And Rowe wasn't going to test his patience.

"There's something going on between me and Vi." Now was the time for radical honesty. Well, mostly. He couldn't make himself air every one of his suspicions about the nature of his relationship with the witch.

"No shit." Gibson leveled a hard look at him. "Do I need to pull you off this job?"

Everything in Rowe rebelled. "I want to see it through." He *needed* to. If Gibson fired him, Rowe would stay anyway. He needed to know what was going on. He needed to keep Vi safe. He didn't trust anyone else, not even his pack.

"Last chance," Gibson said. He picked up his coffee again. "For real this time. No do overs. I want to trust you, Rowe. But you are making it very hard. Do you understand?" Gibson didn't look angry at him. He looked disappointed.

And that was even worse.

Rowe wouldn't say he had daddy issues. He was a grown ass man and he could make his own decisions. But he didn't like the way Gibson was looking at him, and he didn't like the way his boss's disappointment made him feel.

"Understood." Gibson had to believe him.

And he did. "Good. Get out of here. I'll see you later."

Rowe left. Any more time spent with the boss was bound to make things go sideways.

Now he was free to go find Vi.

He reconsidered it for a moment. He had a job to do. She was only *part* of the job. He should have been focused on keeping the entire coven safe. But they had seen the monster yesterday. They had seen the magic tree. She was as much of an asset to him as she was his… whatever. Speaking with her now would be a benefit, both to his job and to his wolf.

Satisfied with the twists and turns in his mind, he headed towards her cabin.

But before he made it, Rosalie stopped him. She looked frazzled and was a bit out of breath, as if she'd been running. Her hair was held back in a loose braid, but some was coming out and framing her face in a dilapidated halo. Her eyes were bloodshot and ringed with dark circles.

"Have you seen Vi?" She sounded panicked.

"I was just going to her cabin," Rowe replied, his heartbeat kicking up. There was no reason to hide it. Especially not if Rosalie wanted him to find her. "What's going on?" He couldn't freak out. But it was disturbing to see Rosalie in such a state.

"She's not there," Rosalie said, gasping for breath. "I've had a portent in my dreams." From any other client, he'd think she was crazy. But she was a witch. "She's in danger. You need to go find her. That other coven. They'll trick her or enchant her. She needs you to keep her safe. She's a target. They'll have taken her into the woods." She nodded behind him. Then she put a hand on his shoulder and squeezed.

She met his gaze and Rowe fell into her eyes. He couldn't look away from her. His ears rang, and he had a strange sense of vertigo.

Vi was in danger.

He had to find her.

He had to save her.

He had to kill anyone who was a threat.

Even as his wolf roared to life inside of him, he shook his head, trying to rid himself of that thought.

Kill?

He'd killed before. He knew what it was to take another person's life. But this wasn't war. He needed to *protect* Vi. That didn't mean he needed to spill blood.

He'd kill the monster roaming the woods in a heartbeat, but he had no desire to take another person's life.

"Find her!" Rosalie got louder and shoved his shoulder. He stumbled back and turned towards the forest.

He had to find Vi. Something was wrong.

He only hoped she knew he was coming.

CHAPTER
TWENTY-ONE

Vi had spent the night tossing and turning, and only half of that was because of Rowe. The other half had to do with what Julian had said to her.

Why did he think she would lure him into a trap?

Needing to clear her mind, she walked along the edge of the camp, not quite dipping into the woods, but far enough away that she was out of sight of her coven. She wasn't going searching for a monster by herself, and she wasn't going to head back to the magic tree.

She just needed to think.

And she hated that it would be easier if Rowe was there with her.

She didn't even know the guy. She'd picked him up from fucking *jail*. Her life did not need a complication like him, and she wasn't about to start depending on him when all there was, was scorching attraction.

You know it's more than that.

She told her mind to shut up. Whatever she knew or suspected was irrelevant at the moment. She had to figure out what was going on. Then maybe her brain would stop spinning in circles for long enough that she could think about what she was feeling for her shifter bodyguard.

Should she go looking for Julian? She wanted him to explain what he meant by his comment, but she was concerned he'd brush her off. Or worse. The binding oath had expired with the sunrise, and now no one was safe.

Vi stopped in her tracks. Was it wise to be so far from everyone else when there was nothing barring Audra Palmer's coven from attacking?

It was too late now. And she doubted someone would be brash enough to attack in broad daylight when she was within screaming distance of the camp.

Of course, if she was wrong, she'd be dead or severely injured.

She'd just have to hope she wasn't wrong.

Had Julian found the magic tree? Was *that* the trap he was talking about? Vi couldn't figure out who or what had created it. It took a massive amount of magic, definitely more power than any single member of either coven naturally possessed, to make something like that. She supposed it could have occurred naturally, or it could be a remnant of some magical tragedy.

But she just didn't know.

Every time she tried to think about it, her thoughts seemed to glide off a slippery surface and plunk her down in some unrelated portion of her mind. And if that part of her mind was thinking about Rowe… well, she'd deal with him later.

She had to talk to Julian. He was the only one who could explain what he'd meant, and maybe if they talked, he'd see that she meant no harm. She wanted this meeting to go well, and she wanted everyone to get along as well as they could.

That meant she needed to do her part.

She pivoted and headed back towards the cabins, but froze in her tracks as a wave of fear washed over her so intense it made bile rise in her throat. She almost doubled over to vomit the toast she'd had for breakfast, but she managed to keep it down.

As quick as it started, the fear morphed into panic and anger.

What? Why?

There was nothing wrong. And yet she wanted to sprint to find the source of it and eliminate it.

Was something wrong with Rowe?

She took off running towards the cabins, but had only made it fifty feet before her wolf came into sight. She felt the moment his eyes locked on hers, and it rooted her in place. His wolf was riding high, she was sure of it. He moved like the predator that lived under his skin and bounded over to her too quickly.

When he got to her, he clamped his hands on her shoulders. His eyes seemed lit by an inner fire and glowed an impossible amber. She couldn't be seeing his wolfish features, not when he was in human form.

And yet she was.

"Where is it?" Rowe demanded. He looked behind her towards the woods, and then clutched her shoulders even tighter and let his gaze rove up and down, taking her in.

"Where's what?" The anger and panic were fading in her, but they still rode high in Rowe. "What's wrong?"

"How did you get away? Are you hurt?" His fingers were strong enough to leave bruises.

"What are you talking about? Let go." She pulled back, but he didn't loosen his grip. Her temper simmered in the back of her mind, but she tried to keep calm. Something was wrong with Rowe. His eyes were full of panic, and it was like he wasn't actually seeing *her*.

"We have to go. You're in danger." He slid one arm around her shoulders and tugged her back towards the cabins.

Vi planted her feet on the ground and refused to move. "What the hell is going on?" She wasn't in any danger. And she was a fucking witch. If there was danger, she could handle herself.

Rowe growled, and it sent a shiver down her spine.

Something was wrong with him. Terribly wrong.

Vi summoned a burst of magic and let it simmer in her hands. "This might hurt. Sorry." She placed her hand on his head and let the magic go.

Rowe howled and stumbled back, clutching his face as the magic wormed its way inside of him, searching for anything that was forcing him to act like *this*. Mind control was a lot easier than people liked to believe, and with so many witches around, anyone could have messed with his head.

"Is everything okay?" She didn't hear Julian approach, and he was lucky she didn't hit him with a bolt of magic. She was on edge.

Her magic should have worked by now.

Most mind control was easily brushed off. If a person knew how to defend against it, it rarely took hold in the first place. But this was more powerful.

This was dangerous.

"I think he's bespelled," she said. Now she didn't have time to ask him about traps, not when her heart was in a vise worried for Rowe.

Julian stepped closer to her, and Rowe straightened, growling and stalking towards him. "She's mine!"

That stopped the witch in his tracks. And it put Vi on edge.

"We need to clear his mind," she told Julian.

He was shaking his head from side to side. "I don't get between mates."

So she wasn't the only one that saw it. The confirmation rocked through her, but she didn't have time to think about it, not when Rowe seemed possessed.

"Please, this isn't him." She might have only just met the guy, but she was sure of that. Rowe could be an ass, but he wasn't this possessive monster. "I just need a bit more power. Will you help me?"

Julian didn't look pleased. He looked one second away from turning around and running back to the camp. Then he held out his hand. "Take what you need."

"Thank you." Vi linked their hands and ignored Rowe's scream of visceral rage.

She summoned power, taking what Julian offered and shaping it to her will. Then she shot it straight at Rowe.

It hit him like an arrow and his eyes widened, flashing purple for a moment before fading to their normal soft brown.

He looked at her in confusion. "Wha—" Then his eyes rolled back in his head and he collapsed.

Her heart stuttered, and if Julian wasn't there, she might have screamed. Instead, he pulled his hand away from hers and knelt down beside Rowe, checking his pulse.

"He's fine," Julian assured her. "Probably just needs a few minutes for the magic to unscramble his brain."

Distantly, she knew that. But it didn't make her heart hurt any less. "Thank you for helping me."

"Do you know who did this to him?"

She shook her head. "He wasn't in a talking mood. If—when he wakes up, I'll ask." She sat beside Rowe and grabbed his hand, lacing their fingers together. His hand was warm. That was good.

Julian stood and looked down at the both of them. "We need to talk. Can you find me after lunch?"

They did need to talk. And Vi should have jumped on this opportunity, but her heart was too busy. She couldn't focus. "I'll find you."

"I'll see you then." Julian walked away, leaving her alone with Rowe.

She was tempted to take him back to his cabin. It would be easier to sleep in a bed. But he wasn't exactly a small man, and she didn't want to invite questions. Dragging an unconscious shifter into the camp would *definitely* raise some eyebrows.

She didn't need to spend much time worrying about logistics. Only a few minutes after Julian left, Rowe groaned and his hand twitched in hers.

The fist that had held her heart tight loosened, and Vi felt like she could breathe again.

Rowe opened his eyes. "What's going on?" He sat up, but didn't pull his hand away. "How did I get out here?"

"Someone scrambled your brain." She had to be business-like. They had to face this threat. If she didn't keep a choke hold on her emotions, she might start kissing him and never stop. "Who did you last see?"

Rowe ran his free hand through his hair. He must have still been a bit out of it since he didn't react strongly to the thought of mind control. "I went to see Gibson. Told him about the bear. Then… fuck. I don't know."

"Gibson couldn't have done this." Fuck it. She leaned in and hugged him. He relaxed into her hold like he was meant to be there. "I'll teach you some tricks to keep witches out of your head."

"Yeah, yeah. That would be good. My head is pounding. And fuzzy. I don't like it." He nuzzled against her neck. "Like this. Like you."

Her heart melted. "I like you too." She kissed him gently. With his brain still unscrambling and the migraine he was sure to have, she couldn't take what she wanted.

But Rowe was going to be okay.

She was going to figure out who had done this to him, and that person was going to pay. No one hurt her mate.

CHAPTER
TWENTY-TWO

Rowe's head cleared after about fifteen minutes, and he was shaking with anger. Someone had messed with his head. He could have hurt someone.

He could have hurt *Vi*.

Everything within him rebelled at the thought. Nothing could compel him to hurt her. And yet she had moved a few feet away from him and had her arms wrapped around her midsection as if she was trying to protect it.

"Are you alright?" he forced himself to ask. He didn't know what he'd do if he'd hurt her. He hoped she could come up with the appropriate punishment.

Vi unwrapped her arms from around herself and shifted closer to him. "I'm not hurt. I'm *angry*."

"I'm sorry." Shame washed over him. "I know I said some things, but it's all kind of blurry."

"Not at you, stupid wolf. At whoever decided to

serve up scrambled shifter brains for breakfast." She curled her hands into fists and took a deep breath. "Do you remember the last person you saw before Gibson? Has anything become clear?"

He shook his head and winced at the sting of his fading headache. "I was coming to find you. That was the plan as soon as I woke up. Someone must have ambushed me." But even as he said it, it didn't ring true. He might not have known everything that came with being a werewolf, but he was a trained soldier. Ambush wasn't easy.

"Or it was someone you had no reason to mistrust."

"Other than my team, you're the only person I trust here." From the way her eyes widened, he wondered if it was too much, but he wasn't going to hide his feelings. "Do you think it was someone from the other coven?" He slid closer to her until their hands were touching. She flipped her hand over to link their fingers together.

Something tight uncurled within him. There. That was right.

"I don't know. If it wasn't for Julian—a healer from Palmer's coven—you would still be under that spell. He loaned me his power. Of course I saw him sneaking around with that shifter, Nora, last night, so I don't know what he's doing. Maybe they were just canoodling." She let out a sound of frustration.

"Canoodling?" Despite the situation, he grinned. "Really?"

"They were standing close! I don't know. This whole thing feels off. I'm trying to figure out why."

She was right about that. Nothing about this meeting was making sense to him. He'd thought it was just witchy business, but apparently there was more to it than that.

"We should head back," he decided. "I want to feel out the other shifters. They might know something."

"I'm going to investigate the camp. Maybe I'll feel a trace of the magic that was in your head. Or maybe Julian can tell me whatever he wanted to say."

Rowe didn't mean to let the growl out, but Vi kept mentioning this Julian guy.

Instead of getting angry, she grinned and cupped his cheek before laying a gentle kiss on his lips. "Don't worry, Mr. Wolf, it's strictly business."

He chased the kiss and captured her lips for his own. But they couldn't sit there kissing forever, no matter how much they wanted. After a few more stolen moments, they separated and headed back to their separate investigations.

It didn't take long to gather all of the shifters together, though Nora West and her team were wary. They met in the recreation building. All of their cabins were too small to hold eight people, and the recreation building was as close to neutral territory as they could come by.

Gibson, Hunter, Owen, and Rowe all sat on one side of the table, while Nora, Estelle Wolfe, Enrique Anderson, and Shannon Reese sat across from them.

"What's going on?" Nora asked after they'd been sitting in silence for a few minutes. "Don't waste our time."

"We thought now is the time to compare notes on this monster in the woods," Gibson answered. The meeting might have been Rowe's idea, but Gibson was their leader.

"It's magic. Shouldn't you be talking to your witches about that?" Nora raised an eyebrow and leaned back in her seat, thought she couldn't lean far, since they were sitting on backless benches.

"Because we all want to keep our witches safe. We thought it best to talk, werewolf to werewolf."

Enrique scoffed, and Nora gave him a sharp look.

"What?" asked Owen. "Is that so hard to believe?"

"You call yourselves *werewolves*?" Shannon's voice was dripping with disdain.

Rowe was confused. "What else would we call ourselves?" Every time he thought he had a handle on the werewolf situation, the rug was pulled out from under him. There wasn't exactly a guidebook for this shit. No matter how much Owen insisted that episodes of *Teen Wolf* could give them insight.

"The correct term is shifter," Nora said with more patience than he would've expected. She gave Shannon a slight shake of the head, cutting off that line of critique. "It's obvious your pack is uninformed. But this level of ignorance could get you all killed."

"You will have to forgive us for our ignorance," Gibson responded, voice dangerously calm. Rowe could feel violence rising close to the surface, but the major didn't give a hint of it. "We were not introduced to this life in any sort of traditional way. At least we don't think so. We can't be sure, *uninformed* as we are."

Nora stared at them for a long moment, assessing them in a new light. The rest of her shifters were still as statues. "Would you care to tell us?"

"No, I don't think I will." Gibson stared right back, face blank.

She nodded rather than push the issue. "Perhaps once this job is done, we could have further discussion."

"Perhaps." Gibson was playing it cool, but excitement bubbled under Rowe's skin. They had taken this job because Rosalie had promised information, but Nora could give them even more than they dreamed of. They just had to hope she was telling the truth.

He had seen Rosalie today.

A shock went through Rowe as the realization

washed over him. Some extra cobwebs cleared, and he remembered his day. First, he had woken up determined to see Vi. Then he had spoken to Gibson. And *then* he had run into Rosalie.

And at some point in all that, his brain had been scrambled.

Had Rosalie done that to him?

Why would she?

He had to talk to Vi. Maybe she could shed some light on the situation.

"You're here to look after your people," said Gibson, catching Rowe's attention once more. "We want to keep our people safe. We need to share resources about whatever threat is out in those woods."

"How do we know those threats aren't coming from your witches?" That jibe came from Estelle.

"We don't want anyone to get killed," said Gibson.

Estelle wouldn't let up. "Your little wolf there is already compromised." She nodded to Rowe, and he glared. "He seems a little too close to your witches."

"And Nora seems very close to one of yours." Rowe wasn't going to stand for that.

The other werewolves—*shifters*–growled at him. Gibson shot a harsh look his way.

He stood down.

"Will you help us get to the bottom of this thing?" Gibson asked again.

Nora wasn't willing to go quite so far. "We will

make sure there's no body count. We can do our jobs."

And that was that. The shifters split up to go guard their charges. But Rowe had another idea.

He needed to find Vi. They had to figure out what Rosalie was up to.

CHAPTER
TWENTY-THREE

Vi set the molar down on the tiny table in her tiny cabin and studied it for several moments. An internet search indicated it probably belonged to a black bear. And her instincts were pounding at her, telling her that it belonged to the vicious monster in the woods. But she had no idea why the tooth had been where it was or how it had fallen out.

That was what she was about to find out.

She took several breaths to center herself and summoned magic from deep in the earth. It floated up into her, making her blood sizzle as power flowed through her veins. She held one hand over the tooth and let her power surround it.

She only wanted information. She didn't want to control the bear. She didn't want to control whoever had enchanted the bear.

But who had done it?

A familiar tingle of magic pulsed at her hand, and it was such a surprise that she almost lost the spell, but Vi quickly re-centered herself and sent another pulse of magic into the tooth to confirm.

That familiar magic tingled back.

Rosalie.

Had she found this tooth first? Had she done her own investigation? Was she looking into who had cursed the bear?

The questions washed over Vi in a wave, but they were quickly followed by darker suspicions.

Did Rosalie have something to do with the cursed bear? And what about the magic tree? Had she scrambled Rowe's brain?

Anger bubbled up so fast that the magic she was channeling turned to smoke, and she cut it off with a harsh flick of her wrist before she could cause any damage to the cabin. Fine-tuned magic required emotional control, and she wasn't about to lose it. But the thought of what had been done to Rowe was nearly enough to make her lose her head.

She wanted revenge.

Why had Rosalie brought the covens to this camp?

Was Rosalie some kind of threat?

Vi backed up from the table, shaking her head in automatic denial. She had known Rosalie her entire life. She was an old family friend. Hell, she was practically a relative. The woman had taught her how to be a witch.

She couldn't be evil.

But she had brought all of these witches out into the middle of nowhere, and Vi still wasn't sure why. She had followed because Rosalie was her coven leader, and that was what she was supposed to do.

But she wasn't supposed to follow without thought. And she sure had been doing a lot of unquestioning following ever since she'd rejoined Rosalie's coven.

Why?

Vi needed to walk. She needed to think. The walls of her little cabin were closing in around her, and she couldn't breathe.

Vi stashed the tooth under a loose floorboard and set a security spell on top of it. The spell would make it so that anyone who was looking wouldn't notice the floorboard, and if they did break through the spell, she would be alerted.

It wasn't perfect, but she needed to move.

It was getting close to lunch, and several of the other witches were out and about. She nodded in greeting to a few of her fellow coven members, but she wasn't in the mood to talk.

Did any of them suspect Rosalie? Could she talk to any of them? Vi needed to talk to someone, but what if they reported back to Rosalie? There was a possibility that she was the only one who didn't know about the dark deeds her coven leader was potentially committing.

She still had to find Julian. Maybe he could shed some light on the situation. And he certainly wouldn't report back to Rosalie.

She wanted to talk to Rowe, too. He wasn't a witch. But he was the one person that she trusted right now. And she was done fighting the instincts that were telling her that he belonged to her.

But where was he?

She didn't have a chance to look.

A hand clamped on her shoulder and tugged her behind one of the tiny houses. Vi whipped around and saw that it was Rosalie.

She tried to keep her expression neutral. She didn't want any of the questions she was grappling with to show on her face. She couldn't accuse her coven leader of what she was thinking. And she feared that if she flat out asked her, Rosalie would lie.

"I'm so glad to see you." Rosalie was a bit out of breath, but her smile *seemed* genuine, though it was tinged with worry.

Vi could feel magic in the air, so she reached into the ground and pulled a little up into herself, leaving a defensive shield around her mind. But even as she did the magic, she faltered. Did she really think Rosalie would screw with her brain? Her trust ran so deep that even shielding herself felt like a betrayal.

She let the shield down for an instant, and then

sense intervened. She put it right back up, her mind only defenseless for a few seconds. Rosalie didn't have to know she was doing it. And she needed to stay safe.

Rosalie let go of her shoulder. "I need your help," her coven leader said.

A sense of urgency shot through Vi, and she leaned in close. "What is it?" Her heart beat fast, and her mind raced. For a second, she was worried, but she had the defensive shield up. Rosalie couldn't get to her.

"You're the only one I trust." Rosalie's voice was low and urgent. "Only you can do it."

"Do what?" Vi looked around to see if there was anyone else near them, but they were alone. "Are you okay?"

Rosalie shook her head, body trembling. "That monster. It's nothing natural. I need you to go out and find it. Find out who's doing this. You're the only one who can."

"Of course." The agreement came out before Vi could even think. Why was she agreeing? That was crazy! She couldn't go and fight an enchanted bear alone. And she was *far* from the only one capable of defeating it.

But Rosalie gave her a little push, and she was stumbling back towards the forest.

Vi's head was fuzzy. What was going on? She was shielded. She should be safe.

She couldn't stop herself from putting one foot in front of the other. She didn't want to go into the forest. This was wrong.

What was she doing?

She kept moving. Tree branches whipped at her head. She made it far enough into the forest that the bright noonday sun was little but a dim memory. There were no bugs making bug noises, no birds, no small creatures.

Vi forced herself to stop. Now that she was deep in the woods she could, as if the compulsion had loosened its grasp just enough for her to think.

And she had the sinking suspicion that Rosalie had done something to her mind in that split second where she'd let her shield down.

She was in the woods now, and she needed to regroup. Maybe she could use this opportunity to find out more about the monster. She could find out if the bear really had Rosalie's magical signature, if Rosalie really was in charge of this.

But why would she send Vi to go out and fight it alone?

Because it would kill her.

It was a swift realization that made her sick to her stomach. Rosalie must have thought she was getting too close. She didn't want Vi defeating the bear, she wanted the bear to defeat Vi.

That wasn't going to happen.

Vi refused to give up that easily.

She reached deep into the earth and summoned as much magic as she could. The trickle was weak, and she feared that both the bear and the magic tree that lurked somewhere in these woods were sucking the natural magic out of the area.

She could rely on the magic that lived within her body, but doing so was dangerous. If she tapped too deep, she would kill herself.

She would rely on the earth until she couldn't rely on it anymore.

Vi walked carefully. She didn't want to stumble on the bear by accident. But she had only made it a few more feet when a loud noise crashed through the woods, and the bear's roar was close enough to deafen her.

CHAPTER
TWENTY-FOUR

Vi wasn't anywhere that Rowe looked. He tried her cabin first, and it was empty. She wasn't in the rec center either. His wolf prowled under his skin, anxious and ready to burst out.

He asked a few of the witches and no one had seen her.

He had the sinking sensation that something was wrong. It only grew worse when he thought he caught her scent at the edge of the forest.

She wouldn't be stupid enough to go in there alone. Not with the power sucking tree and the possessed bear.

Not if she was in her right mind.

But what if Rosalie had gotten to her? Rowe hadn't seen the coven leader in his search for Vi, and he didn't know what he would do to the older woman if he found her and Vi was hurt. No, he knew.

Blood would drench the grass if Rosalie had hurt her.

He needed to find Vi first. He needed to bounce his suspicions off his mate so he could know whether he was crazy or not.

He didn't *feel* crazy. Things were finally starting to make sense.

The smart thing to do would be to go back and talk to Gibson or Hunter or Owen and get someone to go into the woods with him. But panic was beating at the back of Rowe's mind, and he couldn't stop himself from stepping into the forest.

Vi was in danger. A second's delay could be the difference between life and death.

He lost Vi's scent almost as soon as dove into the woods. His senses were slightly enhanced in his human form, but he would be able to follow a trail like it was nothing if he was a wolf.

The forest gave him cover so he quickly stripped off his clothes and folded them neatly beside a tree on the edge of the woods. Then he let the change ripple through him, and he fell to the forest floor with four legs instead of two.

The world around him was new. There were thousands of scents, and he wanted to follow them all. His tail wagged in excitement at the prospect of a hunt, and he almost lost himself to the sensation.

But he'd shifted for a reason.

And now the wolf was in control. He had to find his mate.

Her scent was obvious and he breathed in, letting himself roll around in it for a moment. He wanted to always be covered in her scent just as she should be marked by him. A warning to anyone who would dare get between them.

He followed the path deeper into the forest, each step carefully chosen and silent. He was a predator here, but he didn't want any prey getting in the way. The only person he was hunting now was his mate.

Her scent got stronger as he moved deeper into the woods.

Did she need him?

Did she know he was coming?

Something foul coated the back of his throat, a vile scent that drowned out Vi's lush sweetness and made him gag. No question what that was.

The monster.

He growled. There was no holding it back. In this form, he was too close to his primitive half, and he couldn't stop himself if he tried. His teeth ached to tear into that thing and destroy it for good.

Rowe ran further into the woods, his hackles raised at the way the monster's scent was overlaid with Vi's. He didn't care about scaring prey animals anymore. He needed to move fast.

And when he scented his mate's blood, he howled.

It was a sound of rage, a cry for help. And a warning. The bear would not live to see another night.

The scent of blood got heavier, and it wasn't only his mate's. The vile stench of monster blood was even worse than its natural scent. But it meant that Vi wasn't helpless. She was fighting back.

He heard a crash deeper into the woods and a feminine curse. And then he saw her.

Vi.

Mate.

She sent a weak jolt of magic towards the monster, who stumbled back into a tree and gave a yelp of pain as its fur was singed by her magic.

Rowe didn't think before he acted. He pounced on the weakened bear, swiping his claws against its body and digging his teeth into the soft skin of its belly, ripping out its innards and letting them spill to the ground.

The bear screamed.

If he paused to think, he would know he was crazy. A pack of wolves could take down a bear.

But a single wolf?

Rowe didn't care. The bear swiped out in its dying struggles, and its claws clipped Rowe on the shoulder. He yelped and jumped away. He would have cursed if he had the proper throat.

Vi said something, but he was too focused on the bear to decode what she was trying to say. His wolf ears weren't great at understanding English.

His teeth bared, he stared at the monster as blood poured out of it and it gave its final labored breaths.

It died gasping in pain.

But he wasn't ready to give up on it yet. The thing was cursed. What if it rose like some kind of evil bear zombie? He wasn't going to be caught out by a shambling, undead creature.

He waited. And waited.

And waited.

Time moved differently in this form. He didn't know if he stared at the dead monster for a minute or an hour, but after some time, his mate's fingers ruffled his fur and urged him to back away from the beast.

No matter his form, Rowe couldn't resist his mate.

"You're hurt," Vi said. She wrapped an arm around him, careful to avoid the worst of his injuries. Her skin was soft but not nearly warm enough. He could tell, even through his fur. He needed to warm her up.

Rowe wanted to nuzzle into her soft flesh and let her pet him for days. The danger was past. They could take the moment to enjoy each other. But there were things he couldn't do in this form, things he *needed* to do.

She could pet him later.

And he let go of his wolf, shifting back to man. He didn't care that he was naked. Hell, he wanted his mate to see him naked.

The shift had healed most of the wound, but there were still claw marks on his shoulder and the blood fell in a trickle.

He didn't care.

He wrapped his arms around Vi and pulled her close.

"You're okay," he told her. "It's dead." He couldn't quite latch onto relief at the dead monster. He needed to keep holding his mate, needed her presence to settle all of the terror in his mind.

"You idiot." It wasn't an insult. She was riding the edge of panic, and he could hear the affection in her tone. "You attacked a fucking bear."

"And I would do it again," he promised. He hadn't given a single thought to his own life, not when he needed to protect Vi. She had to know what she was getting into. But she didn't have a choice. He was past the point of letting her go.

They pulled apart just a bit, and Vi ran her hand over his shoulder. "It's not as bad as I thought." She placed her hand on top of the wound and it tingled. "Just a bit of healing," she told him.

Rowe cupped her cheek and their eyes met. His heartbeat kicked up, and his blood hummed. This woman, this witch, was his, and he'd do anything to keep her. Send in the bears, he'd fight them all to prove himself.

He leaned in close and captured her lips. A thank you for the healing. An affirmation of survival. A declaration of intent.

A claiming of his mate.

CHAPTER
TWENTY-FIVE

The kiss rocked Vi to her bones, and she clutched tight to Rowe, unwilling to let him go. It was only when her fingers splayed against his naked back that she realized he wasn't wearing any clothes, and that shocked her enough to make her step back.

Not that she had any reason to complain about a naked Rowe.

His eyes glowed that impossible shifter gold and he watched her, his wolf still close to the surface and ready to pounce. That look sent a shock of heat through her body.

She wanted to be devoured by this man.

Her eyes flicked down, taking in his naked body, and she couldn't look away from his sculpted muscles and his well-formed... everything. She wanted him. All of him. Right now. Her body was hot and tight and empty, but a foul smell tickled her nose and she was forced to glance over at the fallen bear.

Hell of a mood killer.

"So that was a monster?" Rowe asked, his voice a bit rough and rugged, as if he was getting used to having human vocal cords again.

"Looks like." She took a step closer to the beast and heard Rowe growl. She looked back at him and glared. She didn't have time for shifter protectiveness, no matter how much the growl made her shiver. "Do you want to know if it was a monster or not?" she demanded.

"What if it rises from the dead?" he asked, tone utterly serious.

His ignorance about magic knew no bounds. "It's not a fucking zombie. It's dead." She was almost certain of that. Zombies didn't exist. And it took a lot to reanimate the dead.

But once he'd put the thought in her head, she couldn't stop worrying, and she was cautious as she closed the distance between herself and the dead bear. The magic in the ground was still weak, and she could only pull a trickle into herself, but it was enough to scan the bear and find something.

And that something made her sick.

"What are you doing?" Rowe rushed forward as she went to her knees and stuck her hand inside the bear's mouth.

"Witchy business. Trust me." The bear's mouth

was still hot and slimy with saliva, but it didn't take long to find what she was looking for. And right where a molar should've been, she found the charm embedded in the bear's skull. She didn't have to pull very hard to yank it out.

"What the hell is that?" The question didn't come from Rowe. It was Hunter, one of the other shifter bodyguards who had just joined them. Vi and Rowe had been so caught up in each other and the bear that neither of them had heard her approach.

But Vi wasn't about to let the new shifter distract her. "It's what was controlling the bear." Vi turned and rose from her knees, displaying the piece of green rock that had been where a tooth was supposed to be. "Magic charm."

"We've been terrorized by a black bear with a toothache?" Hunter demanded. She glanced at Rowe, careful to keep her eyes above anything private, and then she grinned. "Never mind. I've seen these guys when they experience the slightest inconvenience."

"Hey!" Rowe's jaw dropped in affront, and he threw his hands up at the insult.

Maybe Hunter wasn't all that bad. Her mate and his friends could probably do with a little teasing.

But she didn't like that Hunter was standing so close to a naked Rowe. She took a step closer to her mate and tried to be subtle about it, but Hunter must have realized what was going on, since she stepped back.

"You're going to be just like Andre, aren't you?" Hunter asked Rowe with a roll of her eyes.

"How bad is he?" Vi had met Andre and Mercy when the heat of the mating urge was riding them hard. But she hadn't heard from them since. Who knew if it had cooled off?

Hunter heaved a sigh. "Well, he hasn't peed on her to mark his territory, so that's good. But I would keep a spray bottle around just to discourage any negative behavior from this one." She jerked a finger at Rowe.

"I outrank you." Rowe glared at her.

"We haven't been in the military for years," Hunter responded.

Yeah, she and Vi could be friends.

And maybe a spray bottle wasn't such a bad idea. She had a feeling Rowe liked to leave his towels on the floor.

She forced herself to look back at the gem in her hand. There was nothing particularly special about the green rock. It wasn't emerald. It might have been jade, but she wasn't sure. The appearance wasn't the important part. The power swirling within it was.

"Is that what's been causing all of these problems?" Rowe asked. He looked over her shoulder, the heat of his body on the edge of distracting as she studied the magic relic.

Vi forced herself to focus on the task at hand. But even with the dead bear so close to them, Rowe smelled *good*. "From the bear, yes. From the tree? I don't know." She pulled on more power and let it surround the rock. And she wasn't surprised when she recognized the magical signature.

Rosalie.

Her stomach lurched at the betrayal. She looked up and met Rowe's eyes, and he understood without her saying anything.

He wrapped his arms around her in a tight hug, his skin hot and comforting. "What do we do about that?" he asked.

Vi wished she had an answer. Or at least an explanation. "I don't know. It doesn't make any sense. Maybe she's being controlled?" She wanted that to be true, even as she knew it couldn't be. Rosalie was too experienced of a witch to fall for something like that.

And she had done mind control against Vi.

Why would she do that? She had sent her to be killed by the bear.

"What's going on?" Hunter asked. She took a step closer to them, but not close enough that she could clearly see the gem in Vi's hand. And that probably had to do with the possessive hold Rowe had on Vi.

"Rosalie is up to something," Vi said and felt the finality of that punch through her like a fist.

"I was coming to tell you," Rowe added, squeezing her once more before loosening his hold. "I remembered seeing her before my brain got all scrambled. I think she did it to me."

Vi's shoulders slumped, one betrayal piling on top of another. She wasn't surprised.

"We have to tell the others," said Hunter. She was all business, and that bolstered Vi. There was no time for feeling sorry for herself, not when potentially everyone was in jeopardy.

"She sent me here to die. What am I supposed to do with that?"

Rowe was quiet for a moment, and then he kissed her forehead. "I have an idea. I don't think you'll like it."

CHAPTER
TWENTY-SIX

They managed to get back to Rowe's cabin without catching the attention of any of the other witches. There was barely enough room for the three of them. Vi had unclasped the bed from where it was secured against the wall and was sitting on it. Hunter was wedged into the tiny sliver of kitchen where she could stand, and Rowe decided to sit next to Vi on the bed.

"Owen and Gibson are busy," Hunter reported. "That's why I came for you alone. They're out doing a security sweep."

"Apparently we'll need to be protected from the people who hired you." Vi slumped back against the wall of the cabin and pulled her legs in close. She'd kicked off her shoes when she sat on the bed, and Rowe was charmed by the fact that she was wearing socks with smiling ducks on them.

"We'll loop them in later," said Rowe. Gibson wasn't going to be pleased. Just another way he'd managed to screw things up.

"So what's this plan that I'm going to hate?" Vi still sounded shaken, but she was ready. And she was right next to him. The heat of her body was a welcome presence.

"Lord save us all from Rowe's ideas," Hunter muttered.

Rowe glared at her. "I have good ideas." Not that he was going to waste time listing them.

"How many arrests do you have to your name?"

Unfair. "Those don't come from bad ideas. They come from self-destructive tendencies. Pay attention."

"You sure you want to deal with that?" Hunter turned to Vi with a concerned look.

He growled at Hunter, and she just grinned at him.

Vi reached out and grabbed his hand, lacing their fingers together. "Yeah. As weird as that sounds. So what's this idea?"

The time for banter was over. But his wolf was comfortable under his skin, satisfied with the way Vi was touching him, claiming him.

"Does Rosalie know that you killed her pet monster? Does that magic thingy tell her what you did?" Rowe really wished he had more knowledge about magic and werewolves and everything important, but he was working on instinct. At least his instincts were usually sharp.

Vi pulled the gem out of her pocket with her free hand and placed it on the bed in front of them. She shook her head. "I don't think so. It takes a lot of power to maintain a connection, especially with an animal. Humans are easier. Similar brains. We know how we think. Animals don't think the same way as humans. There might have been another charm to tell her something bad happened to the monster, but I didn't sense one. At the moment she probably doesn't realize what happened."

There were a lot of *ifs* and *probablies* in that statement, but Rowe would have to work with it. His instincts hadn't steered him wrong yet. "Then we keep you out of sight. If Rosalie thinks the monster either killed or injured you and you're stuck in the woods, maybe that will lull her into a false sense of security. And then we can lure her into a trap."

"And then she will use her magic powers to blast us to kingdom come," Hunter interjected. "We're not dealing with guns here. And I don't have a magic wand."

Red tinged Vi's cheeks, and Rowe grinned at the memory. At any other time, he might have made a comment, but he was pretty sure Vi wouldn't appreciate it at the moment.

Red already fading, Vi turned to him, her doubts

clear. "She won't buy it for long. And where you expect me to hide?"

"You can stay here," Rowe offered. And there were no ulterior motives associated with that. His wolf grunted inside of him.

Yeah. Completely selfless.

"One person looks in the window and they'll see her," Hunter, the killjoy, had to point out.

"Can you magic that?" Rowe asked Vi.

She was already shaking her head. "Any of the witches would sense the magic. And magic tends to carry the signature of the caster. That's how I know Rosalie did this." She pointed to the gem. "It would be better if I just hid under the covers."

"You can do that too." He probably shouldn't have grinned when he said it. Really, she was going to think he only wanted her in his cabin so she'd sleep in his bed.

Which he wanted. More than he'd wanted anything.

Ever.

But *this* was about keeping her safe.

"Why do you want her to think that I'm incapacitated?" Vi asked. She ran her finger over the gem absently.

Because he wanted Vi safe, protected. But he couldn't say that. If she knew his motives were about protecting her instead of catching Rosalie, she'd never go along with it.

Rowe made his pitch. "Because I'm hoping that she will let her guard down. We can look for incriminating evidence if she thinks she's getting away with everything. We can talk to Audra Palmer's coven and see if they can help."

"No," Vi cut him off. "I know that Rosalie is looking really evil right now, but I don't know that other coven. I don't know if they're trustworthy. Just because Rosalie can't be trusted doesn't mean the other people can be. We have to keep this between us."

Hunter made a sound of frustration. "I don't see how that works in the long run."

"Give me a few hours. I'll stay out of sight like Rowe suggested." He tasted victory for a second, but Vi kept talking. "Hopefully that gives us enough time to come up with a more concrete plan."

"I'm in," said Rowe. A few hours of respite was better than nothing. And he could convince her to stay hidden away longer if the plan seemed to be working. He just needed to find a way to keep eyes on her. "And you know we'll help you however you need it."

"I'll go find Owen and Gibson," said Hunter, making her way for the door. "I'm coming back in an hour. Make sure you have clothes on by then."

CHAPTER
TWENTY-SEVEN

Anger and need. Those were the emotions swimming in Vi's heart as the door closed behind Hunter, leaving her alone with Rowe. She wanted to burst out of the cabin and hunt Rosalie down, extracting answers from her, doing whatever it took.

At the same time, she wanted to argue with Rowe that staying hidden wouldn't solve anything. At best, it would delay their problems for a few hours.

But most of all, she just wanted Rowe.

He was looking at her, eyes gone dark with need. There was no hiding that a predator lived under his skin. *Her* predator.

Taking things further than they'd already gone could lead to heartbreak. Even if Rowe was ready to claim her as his mate, they lived in a dangerous world. They'd already stumbled into a dangerous game, and there was no guarantee that they'd make it past the weekend.

Thinking of forever could hurt her more than any spell ever could.

And yet, when it came to this man, she couldn't resist.

"You're thinking heavy thoughts." Rowe's breath came in heavy, strong chest heaving as if standing still. Keeping any distance between them, was as difficult as lifting a thousand pounds.

"It's been a heavy day." At any other time, she might have used this hour to regroup. But she had Rowe. They were alone. And they had a bed right there, ready and waiting for them. "Help me forget?"

He surged forward, arms holding her tight as his mouth crashed against hers. Rowe kissed like he couldn't breathe without it. He was a tidal wave crashing over her and she had to let herself be swept away. There was no fighting against that kind of force.

Vi didn't want to fight him.

She loved the feel of his hair under her fingers as she clutched his head. His beard rasped against her cheek. He was all sensation, lighting her body up and making her desperate for more.

And his taste… that was imprinted on her soul forever.

His aura wrapped around her, body and soul

consumed by this man. Any thoughts of walking away were long gone. Had it ever been an option?

No, she'd sealed her fate in that first moment.

And now she didn't regret it. She wouldn't let herself, not when everything within her aligned and screamed that *this man* was her best choice, her only choice.

Her mate.

She wanted skin. She wanted all of him. Their clothes were a barrier she was tempted to turn to ash with a flick of magic, but even in her lust-frenzied state she wasn't *that* reckless, if only because she worried she might accidentally singe one or both of them in the process.

Clothes came off in a flurry. Shirts, shoes, bra.

Pants.

They ripped at each other, battling garments as if they were enemies on a battlefield. The sun was starting to set outside and the cabin was bathed in a golden glow, making Rowe look like her own personal sex god.

She wanted to devour him. Worship him.

Keep him forever.

It was fast, but that didn't matter. That was what mating *was*. And when they were together like this, there was no room for doubts. She didn't know if she'd ever feel a doubt again.

Rowe backed her up until her legs hit the edge of the bed and pushed her down. They hadn't magically found more room to maneuver in the tiny cabin, but it didn't matter so much when they were trying to be as close together as two creatures could be.

He sank to his knees, and Vi's heart flipped. And when he nudged her legs apart, her body went up in flames.

Yes.

He devoured her, showing no mercy as she writhed under his tongue, too caught up in sensation to do anything besides beg for more. The man was a master, a savant, and she was his. All his. No argument when he could bring her to the highest highs with his finger and his mouth, as if he'd been designed just for her.

Her fingers tangled in his hair, holding him to her, not that he needed even more encouragement. She got the feeling her mate could live between her thighs for days without complaint.

She wouldn't be complaining either. And it wouldn't take her long to lose the ability to speak altogether.

She gasped as he changed his angle, focusing on the seat of her pleasure and sucking, making her practically jump off the bed in a wave of shocked ecstasy. Release ripped through her, her body rippling around Rowe's tongue as he had his wicked way with her.

The man was a menace, the kind she wanted with her always.

She tugged him up. She could let him stay on his knees all day if they had the time, but in the back of her mind she knew they'd have company soon enough, and they'd need to face the real world.

Until then, she was going to steal every second with this man.

When she kissed him, she could taste herself on his lips, and as she leaned back and he came down on top of her, his thick cock brushed against her stomach. She felt empty without him, her body yearning to be filled by her mate.

She wrapped a leg around his waist, pulling his body even closer and luxuriating in the feel of skin on skin.

This was how it was supposed to be, just the two of them pressed together, the heat of their bodies an inferno that threatened to melt everything around them.

Vi sent out a lick of power, and above her, Rowe groaned. "What the fuck was that?" he asked, words roughened with pleasure.

"Did you like it?" She sent another wave of magic, and somehow his cock got even harder.

Yeah, she guessed. He did.

"Fuck, it's like you're touching me *everywhere*. How are you doing that?"

She grinned. "I'm a witch, baby. Don't you forget it." She sent one more lick of power his way, this time wrapping it around his hard length and holding it until his eyes turned gold.

"You're going to pay for that."

"Do you promise?"

He kissed her again, and no magic in the world could rend control of it from him. Not that Vi wanted to. He kissed like sin and sensuality and she wanted all of it, everything that he could possibly give her.

And then his fingers teased her entrance, and all thoughts of magic flew from Vi's mind. He was weaving a new kind of sorcery with his fingers, something that had her caught up in his spell forever. No magic could break her free. She'd fight any spell that tried.

She was already wet, so ready that she almost begged. But Rowe took his torturous time, sadist that he was. And by the time he nudged her open, she was babbling out promises that made no sense.

If she had secrets, they would have been his.

But she was his already.

And as he slid into her, she held on, moving with him and savoring the way he filled her body like he belonged there. His scent overwhelmed her, green and foresty, with a hint of something charred at the back of it. It wrapped around her the same way his body did, marking her as a part of him.

The same way he was a part of her.

She would never get enough of this man. There was no force in the universe that would pull her from him. She clutched his shoulders, marking him up, definitely leaving bruises. And though they would fade, she was sure he could feel them deep in his aura.

Her power hummed in satisfaction. This joining was more than just sex, more than pleasure. This was a declaration of fate.

Vi surrendered to it. And as their pace increased, all she could think about was Rowe, and pleasure, and forever. And as they crested the wave together, she held on tight and made a promise to the universe.

She was never letting him go.

TWENTY-EIGHT

They still had a little time until Hunter was supposed to get back, and Vi was in no rush to put her clothes on. Rowe held her tight in his arms, and she traced a line up and down the muscles of his chest. Damn, the man had nice muscles.

"Don't tell me you only like me for my abs," he teased, covering one of her hands with his own and pulling it up so he could kiss her fingers.

She splayed her free hand over them. "It is a plus, if I'm being honest." She smiled up at him. Her life was in upheaval. The one person she thought she could trust most in the world was probably evil. And yet she was here cuddled up next to a shifter who fate said was her mate, and she was smiling.

At least not everything to come out of this week was trash.

"What happens if Rosalie really is the big bad?"

Rowe asked. He played with her fingers, finally lacing their hands together.

Her chest ached to think about it. "I don't know. Normally you report bad witchy behavior to your coven leader, and she calls in the proper authorities."

"There are proper authorities?" He sounded surprised.

She had to wonder how he and his people had survived so long when they knew next to nothing about the paranormal world. "Yes. What you think we do? Just kill anybody who crosses the line? That's kind of insane." But Vi wasn't going to go into all of the ins and outs of magical justice at the moment. "I'm not sure what you're supposed to do when it's your coven leader who might be doing the bad stuff. And I'm really worried about what happens when we try to leave. We're isolated out here. She could cause a lot of damage."

She thought they were as close as they could get, but somehow Rowe pulled her even closer. "I won't let her hurt you."

"You'll try." She couldn't feel optimistic about what would happen with Rosalie. Not when she knew just how powerful the woman was. And the ruse about Vi's death or injury couldn't last. Eventually Rosalie would check in on her creature. They needed to get ahead of her.

"I may not be good at much, but I *am* good at my

job," Rowe assured her. "It's not all bar fights and motorcycle chases."

"There was a motorcycle chase?" She vaguely remembered hearing an officer say something about that at the police station, but given all of the upheaval, it had slipped her mind.

He shook his head, face scrunched up in comical denial. "Half a chase. Barely even speeding."

And there was the laughter again. Vi never wanted to get out of this bed. "Ah. Share." She wanted to know. She wanted to find out every single one of Rowe's secrets. They'd shared their bodies with one another. She was almost entirely certain that this man was her mate. And yet she worried that if she asked him about the deeper things, he might turn away.

"I thought I was gonna be career military," he said, his voice taking on a distant tone as if he was looking back into the past and reassessing everything. "Twenty years at least. Maybe more. Military family, you know? We're not close. Which is probably a good thing. When I got drummed out after the whole magical wizard/werewolf thing, they weren't happy. They thought I did something wrong. I haven't spoken to them in nearly three years." Vi's heart ached for him. He said it matter-of-factly, but she sensed this was a wound that ran deep.

He continued. "My parents are tough people. And I was their only child. The one they wanted to sculpt into the perfect soldier. It kind of made me not great following orders. I knew as soon as I signed up that it was a mistake. I was just waiting for my contract to be up. Then all of this happened. And what do you do after you're turned into a werewolf —I'm sorry, *shifter*—when you didn't even know magic existed? I just wanted to test the limits of my abilities. And it turned out I haven't found the edge yet."

Vi would give just about anything to speak to her mother one last time, and she couldn't imagine what it felt like to be so estranged that three years could pass without a word.

But since they were sharing… "I have no idea what I'm doing with my life." It was her deepest, darkest secret, and it felt so good to say it out loud.

"What?" Rowe looked confused. "You're so put together. You've got magical powers!"

"The magic isn't that special when you've grown up around witches." And she'd never been the strongest or most skillful witch. But they didn't need to go into that yet. "I tried grad school and that didn't work. I tried following around a rock and roll tour. I met some cool people, but that's not my life either. And then I came back here and I don't know what I'm doing. I want to help people. I think. But now the one thing I thought that I could come back to, that I could trust, it's all going to go up in smoke. Or I'm going to be kicked out of the coven. Because if I'm wrong about Rosalie, she's never going to be able to trust me. And I'm never going to be able to trust her." And yet she still wished deep in her heart that there was some way Rosalie was innocent.

"Well, I'm glad were both such well-adjusted people," Rowe said with a sardonic laugh.

"You're an asshole, aren't you?"

He grinned. "Yup." He popped out the P on the letter. "And you're stuck with me."

"I am?" The grin that bloomed on her mouth almost hurt; despite everything else, she was happy to be in this man's arms.

His grin stayed strong. "Hey, I don't make the rules. I barely understand them."

"I thought you didn't like rules," she teased.

He leaned in close, his lips brushing right over hers. Vi wondered how much time they had left before Hunter was supposed to come back. Surely they could sneak in another round.

"I'll teach you the rules," she promised.

"Let's make our own." He kissed her then, and she wrapped her arms close around him. Her sated body wasn't so sated anymore.

But before they could go any further, there was a knock at the door.

CHAPTER
TWENTY-NINE

Rowe's wolf growled at the interruption, and the animal within him surged under his skin, fighting to break free.

Vi placed her arm on his bicep and gave him a quick squeeze. "Down, boy. It's fine."

"I just want you," he said. He'd never been one to declare his emotions so easily, but with Vi they were right there on the surface, and he couldn't do anything other than be honest.

She smiled, and there was a promise of heat in her eyes, a promise he was determined to claim later. "It's probably Hunter. We have work to do." She pushed the blankets back and swung her legs over the side of the bed. "I'll get dressed. Put on some pants and answer the door."

It was only as he had his hand on the doorknob and was pulling it open that he remembered that Vi was supposed to be hiding, but if it was Hunter, it didn't matter.

It wasn't Hunter.

It was the witch. One of the witches. The male witch. Rowe wracked his brain for a name. Julian, he finally remembered.

"Oh!" Julian exclaimed as he caught sight of Vi shimmying into her pants in a shadowy corner.

So much for that secret.

A growl rumbled deep in his throat. No one got to see his mate naked except for him. "What do you want?" It came out rough, the words barely human. His wolf was ready to pounce, and he had to keep a tight grip on those instincts.

Julian held his hands up. "Hey, I'm not here for her. I just wanted to know if you had seen Nora."

Rowe glared. "She's not here. Do you think I'm hiding her?" He sounded angry, but he couldn't stop it. He closed the door a bit to make sure Julian didn't catch another glimpse of Vi.

But Julian didn't back down. He pushed in further, leaning his shoulder against the door. "No need for argument. I'm just looking for Nora." He sounded a bit panicked.

Rowe took as much pity as he could manage. "She was fine this morning. I saw earlier. But that was a few hours ago." He shut the door in the witch's face before the man could ask anything else.

"That was rude," said Vi, perched on his bed, right where she belonged.

"It's not like we're friends," said Rowe. His mood had swung something possessive, and it was dancing up to the edge of violence. His mate was in danger. They were all in danger. He didn't care if some strange witch was looking for a different shifter.

"I've been thinking…" Vi began, voice trailing off as if he was going to fill in whatever she was thinking.

Rowe's wolf paced under his skin. He didn't like the sound of that. "When? In bed?" His tone was antagonizing, and from the quick glare that Vi shot him, she could hear it.

"No. I was thinking when you were speaking to Julian. And it's been percolating in the back of my mind since we got back here."

He really didn't like the sound of that. "What?" Caution was key here.

"Hiding out here isn't going to work," she said. "Julian just saw me. He could tell anyone that I'm here. I think I need to talk to Rosalie."

"Absolutely not." The command came out before he could think twice. He wasn't letting his mate go into a situation like that. "She scrambled my brain earlier. She sent you to die. You can't just go talk to her." They didn't know Rosalie's endgame, and she was the kind of threat they couldn't predict.

Vi shot up off the bed and stalked towards him.

"You don't get to tell me what I can and cannot do. That's not how this," she waved her hand between the two of them, "works." She adjusted her clothes and turned to grip the edge of the kitchen sink. "She won't be able to get into my mind again—"

"Again?" His claws wanted to tear out, and he needed to hit something, preferably Rosalie. No one got to hurt his mate without payback.

"Again," she repeated quietly. "I'll go in with my shields as strong as they can be. I doubt she'll try to murder me."

"Well in that case, go have a party!" Rowe threw his hands up in frustration. Did his mate want to die?

But Vi wasn't giving up. "Maybe she can give an explanation for all of this. Either we've got it wrong or she'll do a villain monologue or something. We can't just sit around. And you and your people don't know what you're looking for. This is witch business, not shifter business. Especially not..." She cut herself off.

"Especially not what?" he demanded. He was angry at everything, and he knew it was unwise to keep talking, but the desperation for a fight was going to burst out of him one way or another.

She pressed her lips together so hard they turned white.

"Especially not *what*?" he said again, emphasizing each word.

Vi slumped and spoke, each word a barb in his

soul. "You said it yourself, you don't know anything about being a shifter, and you know even less about witches. Maybe I can go talk to Julian and we can team up. He can back me up in confronting Rosalie."

"So I can't protect you, but Julian can." He'd hunt the witch down and show the man just how *protective* he could be.

"Oh my God. Are you fucking serious right now?"

Anger swirled in Rowe's head. He wanted to fight something, but he didn't want to be fighting Vi. He hated the thought of fighting her.

So why couldn't he stop?

She bent down to slip on her shoes. "I need to go think," she said. "And you need to trust me."

"I do trust you," he said. The need to trust her, to let this thing between them develop, was soul deep.

"So why don't you trust my play?" The desperation in her tone threatened to break his heart.

"Because I don't trust suicidal plans." She was being too trusting. Rosalie had already tried to kill her once. Was this some fragment of mind control?

Vi was determined to see it through. "It's not suicidal. She won't kill me."

"You have no way of knowing that." He needed her to understand.

"I can't do this, Rowe. I'm not someone you can just put in a little box and protect. Or a tiny house. I'm going to be part of this. And you can let me act or… Well, you can let me act. Because I'm not going to sit on the sidelines. Get used to it."

She skirted around him and left the cabin.

Rowe watched her go.

A few minutes later, Hunter showed up.

"Where's Vi?" she asked, looking around the tiny cabin as if there was a place to hide.

He hadn't moved an inch, and his wolf was pacing inside of him, begging to be let out. Rowe kept iron control over himself.

"Hell if I know."

CHAPTER
THIRTY

Vi wasn't stupid. And her anger cooled not long after she stormed out of Rowe's tiny cabin. Anger didn't usually take her like that, and it was a surprise. But emotion had a funny way of sneaking up on you.

Given everything that had happened that day from Rowe's run in with mind control, her run in with the bear, to the afternoon spent in bed together, she was a seesaw of feelings.

She probably needed to apologize to him.

But that asshole needed to apologize to her too.

She could feel the potential between them. It could be something real. Something beautiful. But not if they fought like that. She didn't want some relationship that ran between hot sex and hot anger.

She ducked behind one of the tiny cabins and took a minute to think. Rowe had a point about not letting her be spotted. She had to use the element of surprise while she had it.

But she had to get to the bottom of things. Rosalie had never seemed like an evil person before. Why would she suddenly do all these things?

Or was it maybe that Vi didn't know Rosalie as well as she thought she did? She had to do something.

If she wasn't so angry, she would've turned around and grabbed Rowe so that they could go and confront Rosalie themselves. Rowe didn't think that he could fight magic, but a shifter could take a lot of damage. She didn't *want* him taking damage, but she wanted him at her side.

But not right now.

She heard Rosalie's voice on the main path, calling one of her fellow coven members. She peered around the side of the tiny cabin and summoned magic to surround herself. If anyone looked her way they wouldn't see her, not unless they looked really closely.

"Have you seen Vi?" Rosalie asked Delia Cruz. "She wasn't at lunch." Rosalie actually sounded concerned, as if she hadn't screwed with Vi's mind and sent her to fight a monster alone.

And that concern tipped Vi over into certainty. Whatever doubts she had were gone. Rosalie was one of the bad guys.

But who was on her side? And what game was she playing?

"Nope, sorry," Delia responded.

"Strange." Rosalie gave her a nod and headed down towards the recreation building.

Strange, indeed. Did Rosalie really think she should have been at lunch? Or was she confirming that Vi hadn't made it out of the woods alive?

Realization struck. Rosalie's cabin was empty.

If she was going to make a move, now was the time. It was getting dark, and people were probably congregating for the evening meal. She only needed a few minutes to investigate.

Decision made, Vi turned towards Rosalie's cabin, keeping her deflection spell around her. A few witches were heading towards the rec center, but otherwise the path was clear.

Vi sent out a spark of magic when she made it to Rosalie's door, checking for any sort of magical security. She sensed a tripwire and a magical lock on the door. Both were easy to get around, but any of the shifters would have blundered right through them.

Rosalie might have used a magical lock, but she had left the normal lock unlatched. Powerful witches were like that sometimes, completely dependent on magic and forgetting to use conventional forms of security. Today Vi was grateful, as she didn't have any skills in lock picking.

Rosalie's cabin was the biggest out of all of the

tiny houses, but that just meant it had a sleeping loft in addition to the downstairs space. It wasn't actually large. There was a table with papers and candles strewn across it.

Vi could feel magic emanating from it.

In the center of two burning candles was a picture of Audra Palmer, and written in an almost illegible script under it was an ancient spell. Vi could make out the letters, but she wasn't sure what they said. She didn't need to understand it to know that it wasn't good. Malevolence wafted up from the altar.

What was Rosalie trying to do to the other coven leader?

She worked faster. Technically, that altar wasn't evidence of anything. But the stack of papers on the table told another story. There were pictures of Palmer and reports about her movements. Similar reports about other members of her coven were there as well. All of them included information about how powerful they were.

But there was nothing about any sort of negativity. These were threat assessments. Power assessments. But they weren't related to the images that Rosalie had shown to Rowe and Hunter about the disappearing witches.

There was a leatherbound notebook beside the papers, and Vi didn't want to open it. She had a sinking suspicion that she knew what she would find once she did.

She forced herself to move and pinched the edge of the brown leather to open it gingerly. On the first page was an image of one of the disappeared witches along with the power level assessment and a clearly written out list of their comings and goings.

The next page had a picture of a different witch and a different schedule. She flipped through five more pages, and it was all the same.

Rosalie was tracking the witches who had disappeared or been horribly killed, and she knew the power level of each of them. There was no reason to track that unless she was trying to recruit somebody for a coven or preparing to fight them.

Unless she wanted their power.

It was dark magic. The darkest magic. And it was something that could create that malevolent tree out in the woods.

Stealing another witch's magic was worse than killing them, and it took a lot more than a single witch to channel that much power.

Was Rosalie using the coven? Did the coven know?

What had Vi got herself into?

She turned the page again, expecting to find another witch, and froze when she saw a picture of Rowe. That was confusing. It was even more confusing when the rest of the page was written in German. She couldn't speak German. But she reached into her pocket and took a picture. She could always go online and see what an automatic translator spit out.

Did Rosalie have something to do with the reason Rowe and his fellow bodyguards had been turned into shifters?

She'd seen enough. She had to warn Audra that something was going on. And she needed to loop Rowe back in.

Rosalie needed to be removed from power. Whatever was happening, Vi couldn't get to the bottom of it right now. But at least she could warn people.

She spun around ready to leave, and Rosalie was right behind her, outlined in the doorway with magic glowing on her fingertips.

"I should've known the woods weren't enough to take care of you." She threw the magic at Vi and everything went black.

CHAPTER
THIRTY-ONE

"I have to go find Vi." The drive beat at Rowe. He couldn't stand the way she'd walked away. Something was wrong.

Hunter must have felt the same way, given her vigorous nod. "Where you think she went?"

"To talk to Rosalie." His mate was going to kill him someday. Whether she did it herself or by giving him an aneurysm, he wasn't sure, and though he was still angry, he looked forward to it. She was his.

And he had been kind of an ass. He had to apologize for that, and he could do it when she was safe.

"You really think she went after Rosalie?" Hunter pressed. She seemed doubtful.

"No, she didn't go *after* her. She wanted to talk to her." His temple throbbed. This had been one of the longest days of his life, and he was ready for it to be over. He wanted to cuddle up beside Vi and pretend that everything was okay.

"She's not that stupid."

"Don't call my mate stupid." *He* could be angry at her. But he would vigorously defend her against anyone else.

Despite the seriousness of the situation, Hunter grinned. "Your mate, huh?" Her eyes were wide with excitement, and he knew she'd be teasing him the second they had a break.

"Yeah, yeah. We can talk about that later. Let's go find her." And Rowe would take the teasing. Later. Right now, he needed to find Vi.

She had only been gone for a few minutes. He saw two witches going to the rec center, and everyone else must have already been there. The path was empty, and the sun was setting.

There should have been people gathered around making campfires or otherwise enjoying the beautiful night. Was everyone really cooped up in that building?

At least it gave them the opportunity to hunt. He and Hunter headed straight for Rosalie's cabin, and Rowe kept his senses alert.

"Did we pass it?" Hunter asked after they'd been walking for about five minutes.

Rowe looked around and realized they were on the wrong end of the camp. "Fuck." He furrowed his brow and wracked his brain, trying to figure out if there was some sort of magic mojo that had been done to him, but he felt normal. "Come on. Let's go back to the cabin. We'll count our steps this time."

They walked back towards Rosalie's cabin, and Rowe lost count somewhere around five hundred steps. They ended up on the edge of the woods.

"It's magic bullshit," he angrily spat out. "This witchy shit is getting annoying."

"What are you guys doing out here?" Gibson asked, coming up behind them with Owen at his side.

Rowe was glad for the backup. If they were going against a coven leader, he wanted the people he trusted with him. "We're trying to go to Rosalie's cabin," he said. "We think Vi went there."

Gibson pointed over his shoulder. "You mean *that* cabin right there." He didn't ask why Vi would go there; Hunter had already apprised him of the situation.

Rowe looked where Gibson was pointing, and it took a minute for him to realize what he thought was an old woodshed was actually the cabin. Why did he think it was a woodshed?

"Fucking witchy bullshit."

Gibson grinned at him. "You're going to have to get used to it."

Rowe grumbled. But he would happily take it from Vi. Just not anyone else, and certainly not his boss.

With Gibson in the lead, they managed to get to Rosalie's cabin without any trouble.

The trouble was in the cabin. The door hung open, and before he stepped inside, he could smell blood.

Vi's blood.

His hackles rose, and his wolf threatened to surface, but Rowe kept a strong leash on the beast. His mate needed help. He had to give it to her as best he could. And that meant staying human.

For now.

His claws and teeth would tear something apart the second he got the chance.

"It wasn't much of a fight," said Owen. He stood near an empty table and hovered his hand over a small trickle of blood. "There's not much room to maneuver in here, but I would expect more things to be tipped over. I'm guessing Rosalie came up behind her and knocked her out."

Rowe growled. No one held it against him.

"Her blood is mine." He would rend the witch limb from limb for harming his mate.

"Hold steady," Gibson warned, one hand raised in caution. "We need to find her first. We need to figure out what's going on."

There weren't many clues in the cabin. There was nothing on the table, and a quick search didn't turn up any documents or witchy relics.

"Do you think she's hiding it by magic?" Hunter asked.

"It's possible," Gibson allowed. "But we don't have time to try and break the spell we can't even see. I think we need to go and find Nora. Maybe one of the other witches can help. She'll know who to trust."

It had become more than obvious that Rowe and his people were working for the bad guys. He didn't want to seek out any help. He wanted to find Vi's scent, follow it, and rescue her from whatever danger she'd gotten herself into.

But that wasn't possible. And Rowe had to be sane.

For now.

They walked down the central path and peeked into the cabins, but none of the witches were there. The lights were low at the rec center even though it was still early evening, and the place should have been bustling with people eating dinner.

"I saw some witches go in there," Rowe said.

That determined their destination. But when they tried to enter the rec center, it was like some sort of magical force repelled them. The air itself thickened, and they couldn't bust through.

Hunter broke off and ran away as Rowe kept throwing himself at the space in front of the door. She beckoned them over. "Hey guys, over here. I can see through the window."

Rowe would have kept battering the door if it wasn't for Owen's hand on his shoulder. "Come on, buddy. We're going to find her."

Rowe wanted to do violence. He couldn't wait. But he made himself follow Owen instead.

They gathered around the window, and inside, they could see slumped bodies of more than a dozen witches.

"Dead?" Gibson asked. He was grim.

"I see some chests moving," Hunter replied. She was on her tip toes and clinging to the window sill. "I think they're just asleep."

Rowe squeezed in beside Hunter and looked where she was looking. Yes, some of those witches were definitely breathing. He hoped that all of them were breathing. "I don't see Nora," he said. "I see the other shifter guards, but not her."

"Is something wrong?" a male voice asked behind them.

Rowe turned around, teeth bared and growling at Julian.

The witch stepped back in a defensive pose and summoned magic to his hands.

Gibson stepped in front of Rowe and held up a hand to ward off the witch. "Peace," he said. "We think something's up." There was a possibility that Julian was involved in the scheme, but they had to take a risk.

Julian's eyes were narrowed, but he lowered his

hands. They still sparkled with magic, but he wasn't pointing it at them anymore. "No shit. I've been looking for Audra for an hour, but I can't find her. She wanted to talk to me before dinner."

"Have you tried to get inside?" Hunter nodded back towards the rec center.

Julian shook his head. "Audra was planning to eat in her cabin. She in there?"

Hunter and Owen stepped to the side, and Owen dragged Rowe back with him.

"Take a look for yourself," Gibson offered.

Julian approached the window, and when he realized what he was looking at, he gasped. "Are they dead?"

"They're breathing," said Rowe. "Now can you explain what's going on?"

"Nothing good," said Julian. "We have to find Nora. Maybe she can help."

CHAPTER
THIRTY-TWO

Vi's wrists burned, and when she tried to pull them, fire burned into her skin. It was so distracting that it took her several moments to realize she was lying on the dirt. Some of it had got into her mouth and she spit it out.

Rolling over was an issue. She was on her side, and the fire around her wrists seemed determined to keep her there. She stopped struggling against it. She had to figure out what was going on before she wasted more energy.

It was dim all around, the trees of the forest blotting out moonlight. But light was coming from somewhere, and judging by the heat at her feet and the flickers in the air, it was an actual fire.

Rosalie.

The memory of the coven leader's attack washed over her, and Vi remembered that last moment before she'd lost consciousness. Any question of innocence was gone. Rosalie was as shady as they came.

But what was her endgame?

Vi managed to move her head, getting a look around. It wasn't a surprise to see the evil tree that had nearly sucked up all of her magic. But she couldn't feel it. That was bad. She was five feet from that malevolent tower of wood, and wisps of magic should have been teasing her.

She tried to summon magic, but her wrists burned again. Whatever spell held her in place was also preventing her from using magic. Her first instinct was to struggle against it and grab all of the power that lived within her and shoot it out at the magical cuffs, but she forced herself to stay still.

She didn't recognize this spell, but she knew how to bind a witch. And she was willing to bet that any magic she managed to draw would only make the magic binding her stronger.

Vi had to know if she was right, but she was afraid to risk it.

Just one drop, she thought. The well of power inside of her was deep. One drop of magic wouldn't sap her.

She was careful, diving deep into her personal power and extracting the tiniest bit. She shaped it to her will and sent it towards her binding, commanding it to free her.

The fire around her wrists flared, and she bit her

tongue to keep from screaming as the flames flicked against her skin. They were magical flames, and they hadn't been burning her before. But struggle made them burn.

She couldn't break out of them.

Not yet.

Another look around revealed a woman in a white dress now stained with dirt. She was facing away from Vi, but Vi recognized Audra Palmer.

"Hey!" She didn't try to keep quiet. She was at Rosalie's mercy anyway, and the woman would realize she was awake soon enough.

But there was no response. Another look around showed that it was just Vi, Audra, and the fire. Rosalie wasn't there.

She'd be back.

Vi wriggled around until she could see Audra better. Her bonds didn't try to hold her this time. It seemed like as long as she wasn't struggling against them, they would let her move a bit. Her balance was off with her hands behind her back, but she'd manage.

"Audra, wake up!" She wasn't close enough to shake the other coven leader, and for a second, she feared Audra was dead. But the witch's chest rose and fell in a steady rhythm. She was alive. For now.

She heard leaves crunching underfoot and looked that way. Rosalie stepped into the clearing before Vi could even begin to hope she was being rescued.

"You shouldn't have entered my cabin," Rosalie told her. She sent out a wave of magic, and the leaves and branches on the ground piled up into a chair for her.

Vi's bonds flickered. Not long enough for her to do anything, but it gave her hope. Rosalie was extending a ton of magic. If she used too much, Vi might just be able to overcome her bonds.

"You shouldn't have screwed with my mind. Or Rowe's. Or anyone's! What were you thinking? Why did you bring us here? What's going on?" The questions poured out, and Vi didn't try to stop them. Rosalie didn't seem to be in any rush to kill her, so maybe she'd be in a talkative mood.

"Don't act like you've never used magic to confuse a person before, little Vi. I know your sins." Rosalie picked up one of the leaves that made up her seat and crushed it in her palm.

"I've only ever done it to protect my identity or the secrecy of our kind." There were ethical guidelines when it came to that type of magic, and Vi took them seriously. She didn't want to be tempted by the control she could have over other people.

"You think I'm not trying to protect us?" Rosalie demanded. "Our coven has done nothing but grow in strength since I took power. Strength I have shared with every member. Strength I can take from *her*." She sent a lick of power towards Audra, but the woman remained unconscious.

The power around Vi's wrists flickered again.

"You're stealing power?" Horror washed over her. She remembered the files she'd seen in Rosalie's cabin. "You're the one murdering the witches."

The coven leader shrugged, unrepentant. "I'm not the only one."

"Other coven members?" Bile rose in Vi's throat. These people were her friends. They were nearly as close as family. How could they do that?

But Rosalie shook her head. "You're thinking too small."

Vi was having trouble wrapping her head around it at all. "Then what?"

Rosalie didn't answer.

"Come on," Vi cajoled. A part of her truly was curious, but she also knew that the longer she stalled, the longer Rowe had a chance to find her. Their argument was beyond stupid. She wanted to believe it was some of Rosalie's meddling that had caused it, but she was pretty sure it was her own fears that had made that argument happen.

But Rowe would come for her. He had to.

"I want to know," she pressed. "You have me at your mercy. Tell me before you…"

"I don't have to kill you," Rosalie interrupted. She stood, and her magical chair collapsed back into a pile of leaves and branches. "You're like a daughter to me. Your aunt would never forgive me if I let something happen to you."

Unease sparked through Vi, and it made her struggle against the bonds and spark the fire holding her once more. "What are you planning?"

Rosalie smiled, and it made Vi's veins ice in fear. "You've seen how good I am at memory spells." She huffed out a little laugh. "You don't know it, but you've *felt* how good I am at memory spells."

"When you sent me into the woods." It wasn't a surprise. She'd figured that one out herself.

But Rosalie shook her head. "You started asking questions years ago. When you were still in college. I worried you would fight it off when that boyfriend of yours started questioning you. But you never once doubted your own mind. And you won't doubt me when I'm through with you."

Rowe didn't give two shits about Nora, but Julian was frantic to find her. Rowe's wolf surged inside of him, demanding he sprint into the forest and find Vi before anything could happen to her.

Anything worse.

He was kidding himself if he thought Rosalie, bitch witch supreme, hadn't laid a finger on his mate already.

He was going to end the woman and smile while she bled.

"Wait," Gibson said before they could back away from the recreation building. "Do you have any idea what was done to the witches? Poison? Magic?"

Julian vibrated with pent up energy and glared at Gibson. "How should I know? There's a ward around the whole building and it's blocking my magic from entering. Do you think I didn't try to figure it out?"

"Watch your tone," Hunter warned.

Julian leveled an icy look her way. "I'm not afraid of any of you. Now let's go find a real shifter who can find my coven leader."

"Hey!" Owen objected.

Rowe kept his mouth shut. He wasn't sure he could form words right now, and he was just as likely to throttle this witch as anything else.

Nora's cabin was on the opposite side of the camp from where Rowe and his fellow shifters were sleeping. The door was closed, and it was dark inside when they got there. Julian marched up to her door and banged anyway.

"I guess we're not trying for stealth," Hunter grumbled.

"Are you trying to wake the forest?" Nora came from between her cabin and the next one over. "Shouldn't you be in the rec hall? I sent the others on ahead while I was fixing a broken window in Estelle's cabin." She surveyed all four of them. "What's gone wrong?"

Julian jumped off the stairs and crossed the space to her, but froze a foot away and didn't touch her. The air was heavy with something between them, but they didn't exchange a word.

"Everyone in the rec hall is unconscious," Gibson informed her. "They've laid down at the tables, most of the witches from both covens and your people. They appeared to be breathing, but we couldn't enter the building to confirm that it was true for everyone."

"There was a ward," Julian added. "I didn't recognize the magical signature."

"And you all just *happened* to be outside of the rec hall?" Of course Nora was suspicious, it was her job to be suspicious.

Rowe'd had enough. He needed to find his mate. "Rosalie is suspicious as shit. She's gone. We didn't see your boss in the rec hall, and Vi's blood was in Rosalie's cabin. Are you going to help us find them or accuse us of foul play?"

She gave him an assessing look. "I'm sorry if I don't want to run blind into an ambush. You have your mate's scent, why not follow it?"

The suggestion dumbfounded him, and Rowe's wolf surged, wanting to rip through his clothes and change shape right there. But he'd already lost one set of clothes to a shift. He didn't need to lose another. He reached for the hem of his shirt.

"What are you *doing*?" Nora demanded, eyes wide.

"Shifting to follow her scent, like you said." Where was the confusion coming from?

"Your pack really is ignorant."

"We could do without the insults," said Gibson. "We've been flying blind, and we've made it this long. Care to tell us what you mean by scenting her in human form?"

"You're not like any alpha I've met before," Nora said.

Gibson just nodded.

She turned to Rowe, but she was speaking to all of them. "You should always have the full use of your senses. It is sometimes difficult for bitten wolves like yourselves to grasp." Rowe wasn't about to interrupt and correct her about how they'd been changed. "Stop thinking like a human. Let your other self merge with your old self, but don't give into the shift. I have a feeling you're going to want to be two legged when we meet whatever is in that forest."

Rowe didn't want to waste time meditating or whatever Nora was asking while danger waited. Why couldn't Nora catch Vi's scent and lead them to her?

But he wasn't going to put Vi's fate in another's hands. So he blocked out everything except the wolf that lived inside of him.

Okay, pal. Let's do this.

The wolf strained to be let free, and his hands flexed. He could feel his bones trying to shift, but he forced the instinct back. The air around him screamed and his senses were on fire.

His teeth were too big for his mouth, his hands were sharp.

And he had Vi's scent.

He took off running. The others could follow for all he cared. He just needed to find her.

The others must have followed. He could hear them behind him, but he was too focused on Vi's familiar scent to look back to check.

The woods swallowed him whole, and even though the sun had long ago set, he could see like it was noon. The forest was quieter than it should have been, the prey scared away by the predators that stalked within.

He wasn't planning his attack, too driven by instinct to do anything but move. His wolf didn't need a plan. Teeth. Claws. These were all he needed. He'd pounce on the evil witch and end her in one blow.

It had worked on the bear.

But Rowe didn't get a chance. He burst into the clearing and spotted Vi on her knees and struggling. He let out a howl, his human throat struggling with the rage his wolf wanted to let out. The others were right behind them.

The witch was no match for a pack of angry werewolves.

But before they could make a move, she sent a blast of magic at them that sent Rowe and the others crashing to their knees.

CHAPTER
THIRTY-FOUR

Rowe hated magic. It was stupid. And it *burned*.

He couldn't stand. He could barely move. And he couldn't even see the force that was holding him in place. He'd much rather face off against bullets and mortars any day. At least that was a kind of death he understood.

If there was any consolation, it was that Rosalie had turned her attention to him and the others, ignoring Vi and an unconscious Audra Palmer.

He, Gibson, Hunter, and Owen had all been driven to the ground. Julian and Nora were nowhere to be seen. She must have forced the witch to stay back. He had to hope they weren't far behind. Neither Nora nor Julian had any allegiance to Rowe and his people, but they'd want to save their coven leader.

Rosalie got close enough that he could have

swiped out and ended her if he wasn't forced to the ground by magic. And she seemed to revel in it, stepping even closer and laughing when he tried to throw himself at her.

"I think I'll put a collar on you and keep you as a pet." She grinned evilly. "We should have done that from the beginning. What use is it to create beasts if you're not going to keep them?"

"What?" That question was ripped out of Owen, but it could have come from any of them.

Rowe remembered that night in the Black Forest. He remembered being bound and placed in a circle where an evil wizard chanted and performed a ritual he didn't understand. He remembered the mercenaries who had ringed them, the guns a silent threat.

He remembered being shocked that he'd survived.

But he didn't remember Rosalie.

She turned her attention to Owen and whipped out her hand, flicking her fingers up and somehow using her magic to pull him to his feet and then hold him up in the air, feet dangling a few inches off the ground. He struggled against her, but he couldn't fight the magic.

Behind Rosalie, Rowe saw Vi struggle. She was moving around, pulling her hands apart as if they were stuck together with tar. And she was staring at Rosalie as if she could burn holes into the back of her head by the power of hate alone.

Vi *was* a witch. Maybe she could.

Then she turned to him and their eyes met. *Keep struggling.* She mouthed the words, and it was so clear he could almost hear them in his head.

He nodded.

He wanted to watch his mate, but he couldn't risk turning Rosalie's attention back to Vi.

"You weren't there." The words didn't come easy. Whatever magic Rosalie was doing made it feel like fingers were digging into his throat and choking off his words. "A man did this to us."

Rosalie turned from Owen, and he dropped to the ground, gasping for breath. She didn't pick up Rowe by her magic, but behind her, Vi stopped moving.

Keep struggling.

Against the magic.

It wasn't just Rosalie's attention that Vi wanted him to keep, she wanted him to make her use magic. Well, this was going to hurt.

"Do you think a single spellcaster could put beasts into all of you?" Rosalie demanded. She stepped close and leaned down, running a finger over his cheek.

Rowe used all his might to turn and snap his teeth at her.

She sent him flying back with a burst of magic and then dragged him back into place with the same power. "That amount of power was greater than any single person could summon or hold. Do you know how many witches were sacrificed to create you?"

No. But he wanted to. They all wanted answers about their origins. And, as impossible as it seemed, Rosalie had them.

But he couldn't get lost in answers. Not when Rosalie was doing something even more sinister now.

"What do you want with Palmer?" It hurt to speak, to fight against the magic holding him. But if it kept Rosalie distracted, he'd do it all night.

"What does anyone want? Power. I'll take hers while my associates make their own preparations. And soon what was done to you will be a blip. The next monsters we create..." Pure evil soaked into her smile, and she didn't need to finish her sentence.

The thought that she had some hand in his creation made him sick. And they couldn't let her do it again.

Rowe fought against the magic, knowing he couldn't win. If anyone could win this fight, it was Vi. And as much as he didn't want his mate in danger, he needed her skills. The others beside him began to struggle as well, and the smirk slipped from Rosalie's face.

It wasn't so easy to hold four struggling werewolves and a fighting witch.

But she had the upper hand and she knew it.

Rosalie sent a huge blast of power towards Rowe

and his pack, and the power burned. He screamed at the pain, not wasting energy in hiding the hurt. He couldn't fight back against it, and he slumped to the ground, his energy spent.

Behind Rosalie, Vi still struggled. She wasn't free yet.

He'd failed.

A ball of energy flashed from behind Rosalie, but it didn't come from Vi.

Julian had arrived.

CHAPTER
THIRTY-FIVE

Vi was going to kill Rowe for rushing into the clearing without a plan. And then she was going to kiss him better and teach him a lesson about defending himself from evil witches bent on world domination.

His pack's struggle was enough to loosen the magic holding her in place and she fed her own magic under it. Her heartbeat kicked up, the first sign of tapping her internal power. She wasn't worried, not yet.

She wouldn't worry until her eyes started bleeding.

As Rosalie sent a wave of power to quell the shifters, Vi sent her own to the bonds holding her. They didn't quite give. She needed another shot. But the magic had done the shifters in, and they were slumped to the ground.

Rosalie would pay for hurting Rowe.

Then Julian stepped into the clearing and started a magic volley. It distracted Rosalie so completely that for half a second the bindings holding her weakened, and Vi took advantage, flashing her magic out and breaking them.

But she didn't stand up and join the fight. Not yet.

While Rosalie was occupied with Julian, Vi army crawled over to Audra and checked on her. She was breathing, and there weren't any bumps or bruises. She'd most likely been knocked out by magic and would recover in time.

If they defeated Rosalie.

Julian had power, but he clearly didn't have much martial skill. The man was a healer, as she'd seen earlier. But he was giving it all he had.

So she was going to help.

Vi stayed low and placed her hands on the ground. Rosalie had sucked up a lot of magic, but there were still trickles of it waiting to be called up. And she called it. The power flowed into her, sluggish at first, but growing in strength as she found a deeper well of it that Rosalie hadn't tapped.

She left the connection to the earth open. She was going to need all the power she could muster.

She came out of her crouch already shooting energy at her coven leader. Rosalie must have seen it, as she set up a wave of defensive magic at the last minute.

Vi put up her own ward. Rosalie had decades of experience on her and probably had a stack of dark magic tricks. They shot volleys back and forth, and at one point Rosalie rent the ground beneath Vi's feet, nearly sending her into a deep hole.

Vi jumped back and shot her power at a nearby tree, breaking a branch and almost crushing Rosalie.

It didn't work.

Then Rosalie's shields solidified into onyx and the only evidence she was still there was a guttural chanting that raised the hair on the back of Vi's neck and made her stomach roil. She didn't recognize the language Rosalie spoke, but it couldn't be anything good.

Whatever spell she was casting was old, dark magic and it could kill them all.

Vi sent waves of magic at Rosalie's shield, trying to disrupt the spell, but it didn't seem to have any effect.

She thought she saw a furry creature moving in the woods around them, but the shifters were still bound, even if Julian had diverted his magic into trying to free them.

Was there another wolf out there?

If there was, Vi hoped it was on her side.

She tried to pull more power, but it was suddenly

gone. Whatever Rosalie was doing was sucking power out of the earth faster than it could be replenished. If she kept going, this spot would be blighted, forever dead and unable to grow anything.

And she and the others would be too dead to mourn it.

The onyx shield dropped, but Vi still couldn't land a hit on Rosalie. Dark magic infused with pulsing red streaks coated the witch, and Vi knew she didn't want to be hit by it.

Rosalie raised her hands high, and Vi held her ground. She would fight until the last breath. She had to stop Rosalie before the woman could bring more evil into the world. If she died, she died.

She had to take Rosalie with her.

She didn't see what happened, but she felt a body slam into her and take her down to the ground just as Rosalie unleashed the magic, not at where she'd been, but aimed straight for Audra Palmer.

A golden wolf jumped from the shadows and in front of the coven leader, absorbing the dark magic with a yelp.

Rosalie screamed in rage, and it transformed into a shriek of pain. Vi whipped around to see three shifters holding the struggling witch down while Julian stood over them and cast a binding spell.

Rowe and his pack were accounted for, so who was the other wolf?

The question was answered when the fur seemed to melt off of the shifter and left a shivering, naked, and very alive Nora West in its place.

CHAPTER
THIRTY-SIX

Rowe didn't want to let Vi back up. It felt beyond good to have her in his arms once more, and he was worried that if he stopped touching her everything would go to shit again. Every time they parted, things seemed to go wrong.

So clearly they could never be apart again.

His wolf liked that. He'd just have to convince his mate.

She grabbed one of the hands holding her around her waist and gave it a squeeze before attempting to peel it off. Rowe resisted for a moment.

"Come on, big guy, we've got to finish this," she said, only loud enough for him to hear.

It was a struggle, but he let her go. His skin felt hot and his wolf strained to get out, but Rowe clamped down on that instinct. He needed to be human right now.

He forced himself to step away from Vi to check on Owen and the others. Hunter had a gruesome bruise blooming on her face and Gibson was covered in dirt. Somehow Owen looked as fresh as when he'd arrived, lucky bastard.

"Any injuries?" The words had to be torn out of him. Talking was so hard with his wolf trying to take control.

"All good," Gibson reported. His hands were holding Rosalie's arms down. Hunter was sprawled across her chest, and Owen had control of her legs. But it was really the witch, Julian, who had the power.

He glowed with it, a faint blue outline all around him and ropes of even darker blue that connected him to the fallen coven leader. "How's Audra?" he asked, not taking his eyes off Rosalie. "Is she alive?"

Rowe hadn't checked, but Vi was still by the fire. "She's breathing. I think she'll wake up soon."

"Good." Julian paused, and his magic seemed to pulse before he spoke again. "Nora?" There was hope and fear thick enough to choke on in that one name.

"That hurt like a motherfucker, but I'm alive," she said.

Julian whipped around, and Rosalie flailed before Rowe saw Vi send a wave of her own power to back up Julian's.

He looked over to see a naked Nora standing beside the flickering fire. There was no evidence that she'd been hit by deadly magic. She just looked… cold. And after a quick look to make sure she didn't seem to be bleeding or otherwise hurt, he kept his eyes pasted above her shoulders.

Julian took a step towards her, but then forced himself to stop.

Rowe wanted to know what was going on between those two, but more than that, he just wanted this to be over. There was only one witch he wanted to spend any time with, and as far as he was concerned, they could deal with everything else later.

"I'm not sure what Rosalie's spell was trying to do," said Vi. She pulled off the jacket she'd been wearing and offered it to Nora, who pulled it on and mostly covered her nakedness. "She claimed she's been siphoning power, so it might have something to do with that. May I check you out to see if anything is… bad?"

"No offense, but I'm not letting anyone from your coven touch me." She tugged on the jacket as if she was going to give it back, but then pulled it even tighter around herself.

"Then you should have someone from your coven check it out," Vi insisted.

"I can handle things on my own, thanks." Nora knelt by Audra. "She's starting to stir. Let's take both her and Rosalie back to camp and call in the authorities."

"The cops?" Rowe wasn't sure how they'd handle

a witch like Rosalie. She'd bust out of prison like it was made of spun sugar.

The shifter scoffed. "You really know nothing about this world." She looked over at Gibson. "We will talk later, alpha. When this is all settled."

The major nodded.

Rowe wanted to sit in on that discussion. But that was an argument for later.

Audra groaned and sat up with Nora's help. After that, it was only a matter of figuring out how to transport the two coven leaders safely back to camp. Gibson, Hunter, Owen, and Julian handled Rosalie, who was so tightly bound in magic that she couldn't struggle.

Audra was eventually able to stand, and Rowe joined Nora, each of them taking one of her sides and helping her to walk. Vi walked beside them in case they needed any magical assistance.

Unsurprisingly, it turned into a clusterfuck once they made it back to camp. Whatever had caused the witches to sleep had worn off, and Audra's coven swarmed them, demanding answers and taking their coven leader from Rowe as if he meant her harm.

Vi's coven seemed... smaller than Rowe remembered. And he was pretty sure some of them were missing. Allies of Rosalie?

They'd need to be on alert for attacks in the night. But if he were to bet, whoever was aware of what she'd been doing was cutting their losses and running for the hills. Audra Palmer had plenty of powerful witches with her, and now that they knew of the threat, they were more than capable of facing it.

Vi got swallowed up by her people, giving the answers that she knew and trying to calm the hotheads who were already beginning to weave conspiracies.

"Has anyone seen Delia?" he heard her ask. "What about Katrina?"

So he was right, witches were missing.

Rowe hung back, and the rest of his pack joined him once Rosalie had been secured in a makeshift cell in the recreation building. Audra's witches and their shifter bodyguards were standing guard. Rosalie wouldn't be escaping.

He had questions of his own. What had Rosalie been talking about when she said she had a hand in creating them? Could she lead them to the witch who had performed the spell that night? How deep did the conspiracy go?

But he kept those questions to himself. There would be time for revelations later.

He hoped.

Eventually the witches agreed that there would be no more answers that night, but the only way they would agree to walk away was with the swearing of a binding oath. None of the witches gathered would intentionally do harm to each other for at least twenty-four hours.

The shifters couldn't be bound by such oaths, but they made their promises as well.

Vi followed Rowe back to his cabin without a word, and when the door closed behind them, he pulled her into his arms and hung on tight.

He needed to be as close to her as possible. Clothes were too much. Hell, *skin* almost seemed like too much. If there was a way he could merge their cells together until they were one being, he'd do it in a heartbeat.

But maybe he'd keep that to himself. Vi was where he belonged, in his arms, and she didn't seem like she planned to move anytime soon. He wasn't going to scare her away by his desperate need for her.

Her lips brushed his neck, and Rowe shivered, his whole body coming to life. His teeth ached and felt almost too sharp in his mouth, but he ignored the feeling. He focused on Vi and what she was doing to him and how his body responded.

That was all that mattered.

He had her. He wasn't going to care about anything else.

They kissed, and it was like coming home. He let himself sink into it. Vi's kisses were like none he'd ever had before, and he knew he'd never be able to live without them. She was his now, and he wasn't letting her go.

From the way she held him, it wasn't like she'd let him walk away either.

His wolf was satisfied with that.

For now.

They were gentle in removing their clothes, stealing kisses while each piece of fabric fell on the floor. Rowe wanted his mate alone, but for now the privacy of his cabin was all he could give her.

He'd give her everything the second he had the chance.

He worshiped her body with his hands, with his mouth, with everything he had. She was wet beneath him and begging for more.

And still his mouth ached.

She shivered as one of his teeth grazed her breast.

"Oh my, what big fangs you have." She was looking down at him, her eyes bright and playful, but there was something serious lurking there, something she understood in a way he couldn't.

Rowe grazed her again, raking his teeth over the mound of her breast just enough to scrape, not daring to hurt her.

Vi swallowed hard. "I want you to do it," she commanded.

"Do what?" He'd do anything, everything. She was a feast before him, and he didn't know where to start.

"Mark me. Claim me." She paused, and there was an eternity before she continued. "Bite me."

"Won't that…" He let the question trail off before he finished.

"I'm a witch, you can't turn me. And you can't change someone when you're not in your wolf form. You're my mate. Claim me."

He didn't need any more explanation. Rowe's teeth had to be protruding from his mouth, they felt so big, so sharp. And he let instinct guide him as he found the perfect spot on Vi's neck.

His teeth sank in and he tasted her blood. His wolf howled within him, and she held him close to her.

He couldn't think. His body took over and he slid into her, cock moving in her as her taste nearly drowned him. He had to pull his mouth away, and he was shocked to see the red on her neck, even as the wound was already closing.

He could ask questions later. He was too caught up in the feel of her to do more than *move*.

The rightness of the bond between them anchored her to him. He didn't know if it was her soul or her aura or some other witchy secret, but Rowe could feel her deep within, and he knew there was no backing away now.

Not that it had ever been an option.

Pleasure washed over him, and his mate gasped, her fingers holding on tight enough to bruise. She leaned forward and buried her witchy teeth in his neck. She didn't break the skin, but it didn't matter. He could feel her magic searing him deeply, claiming him in her own way.

It was all he wanted, all he needed. And when they were through, he gathered her close in his arms and held on tight.

He had his mate. He could face all the mysteries of the world, as long as she was at his side.

The camp was a mess in the morning. More of Vi's coven members had taken it upon themselves to leave during the night, and Vi had to wonder if they'd been conspiring with Rosalie. She didn't have a good feeling about Delia or Katrina, and she'd have to investigate that once she was home.

But at least Rosalie couldn't spread her evil anymore.

The magical world was relatively small, but they had structure. And justice. Rosalie wouldn't be summarily executed for her crimes. She'd face a tribunal of witches and be able to plead her case. And when she was found guilty…

Well, that was something to face in the future.

In the early hours of the morning, a team of highly trained witches had collected Rosalie, and some of Audra's coven had gone with them to oversee the transfer.

Everyone else was getting ready to go home.

The knock on her cabin door made her jump. She'd barely spent time in her little cabin, but it was where her bags were and she had to pack up.

Nora stood outside. There were dark circles under her eyes, and she was so pale she looked sickly. Vi was very concerned about the magic she'd been hit with, but she didn't offer any assistance. Nora had rejected her once, and she had access to an entire coven. She'd ask for help from people she could trust.

"Come in," Vi invited, stepping back as much as she could.

For a moment, she thought Nora would refuse, but then she stepped inside. "Your shifters are busy so I thought I could give you a message for your mate."

The word *mate* sent a shock through her. But after another night spent in Rowe's arms and the way her heart warmed every time she thought of him, there wasn't a better descriptor. Yes. He was her mate. And she couldn't wait to discover all that was going to happen between them.

"Sure, I can play messenger."

Nora reached into a pocket and pulled out a business card that also had a phone number and email address scribbled on the back. "The main company info is on the front, that's my personal cell and email on the back. Your shifters need guidance if they're going to survive this world. I think we should talk."

"They're not normal shifters, are they?" Vi had met enough shifters in her life that she knew what to expect. And Rowe and his pack didn't play by the rules.

"No," Nora agreed. "They're not."

"Do you think…" She wasn't sure how to ask the question.

"What?" Nora prompted.

"Are they in danger? From what they are, or from who created them?"

Nora nodded. "Certainly. Which is why I'm willing to help."

"I'm going to look into what Rosalie was doing." She needed Nora to know that. Rosalie had almost killed them all. Her magic was still doing something to Nora. And Vi wouldn't let any more evil spread through her coven.

"Will your new coven leader let you?"

Vi shrugged. "There isn't a new leader yet. And I'll cross that bridge when I come to it."

"Her allies are ahead of you."

"I know." But Vi wasn't going to let anything stop her. And she was a better witch than Delia Cruz.

She walked out of the cabin with Nora, who was looking around. "Do you know where Julian is?" the shifter asked.

"I think he left with the others who took Rosalie into custody."

Nora nodded, and though her face was blank, Vi was sure she was trying to hide disappointment. She walked off without saying goodbye.

Thoughts of Nora evaporated when she spotted Rowe swaggering her way, a playful grin on his face. She would have never guessed he'd been fighting for his life only twelve hours before. And if he'd smiled at her like that when she first met, she might have slapped him.

Now she just wanted to kiss him all over.

He stopped in front of her and cupped her cheek, his grin turning into a soft smile as he leaned in and took one kiss and then another. Vi wanted to surrender to those kisses, but if she did, they'd never get out of the camp.

And she wanted to go home.

"Let's go back to the city," she said.

Rowe kissed her once more and pulled away. "I thought you'd never ask."

The drive back was quiet, but peaceful. She held Rowe's hand for a long time and really let herself believe that this man would be by her side for all the challenges to come. Those challenges would be daunting.

But with him as a partner she could face them.

She didn't bother to ask him whether he wanted to be dropped off at his own place, and he made no mention of it when she pulled into a parking spot near her building. Once they got into her apartment, he let out a low whistle.

"Nice place," he said. "Let me stay tonight and I might never leave."

She locked the door. "I may not have a problem with that."

Then she kissed him.

CHAPTER 38

Two Weeks Later

Vi's desk was covered with the papers she'd recovered from Rosalie's apartment. Luckily Delia and Katrina, assuming they'd known about Rosalie's crimes, hadn't gained access to her apartment.

The wards around her door had taken more than a week to break. Vi might have been able to do it faster if she had help, but she wasn't sure who in the coven could be trusted. No one was.

They had no leader and no one wanted to step up. Other covens in the area were starting to recruit. Vi doubted the coven would survive.

But that wasn't her primary concern at the moment. Rosalie had stacks of files, many innocuous, but some brimmed with the crimes she'd been committing. And the conspiracy went deep.

She hadn't been lying when she said that she

wasn't the only one stealing power from innocent witches. There were at least three other witches siphoning power on the East Coast. Around the world, there could be dozens.

She didn't have names, but she knew who some of the victims were, and that was a place to start.

"That's an impressive murder board," Rowe told her, coming out of the bedroom.

Vi's eyes flicked up and down, taking in her mate. "That's an impressive suit."

"I promised Owen and Stasia I'd go to this stupid luncheon. You can always come with me." He looked so hopeful.

She probably shouldn't take glee in disappointing him. "My tux is at the dry cleaners."

His guttural growl sent a shiver down her spine and warmed her to the core. "You'd look fucking hot in a tux."

"I know. That's why I have one." Fuck, she wanted to rip his clothes off and take him right there. But Owen and Stasia were on their way, and the last time he'd been delayed because of... activities... they'd been teased for days.

Mating was exhaustive work.

To distract herself from her tempting mate, Vi turned back to the table and grabbed Rosalie's date book, opening it up to a random page. A slip of paper nearly fell out, and she slammed her hand down on it to save it.

"Easy there, tiger," Rowe warned. He came up beside her. "What's that?"

"I don't know." She set the paper back down, and Rowe cursed.

"That's a fucking ticket stub. From a flight to Germany." He reached for the ticket, but Vi stopped him from picking it up. He sounded angry, and she couldn't risk him tearing the thing up.

Not that he would, but shock made people do stupid things.

She kept the stub on the table and studied it. "Stuttgart. Two and a half years ago. Does that add up with when you were taken?"

Rowe nodded. His face had lost color. Vi reached out her hand and used magic to tug a stool closer to the desk so he could sit. He sank onto the chair as if his muscles were melting.

"You okay?" She gripped his arm and squeezed, trying to ground him in the moment. It was hell knowing a woman she'd trusted had been involved in so many evil schemes, but she'd been neck deep in discovering Rosalie's wrongdoings for weeks.

Her mate nodded. He pulled her hand off his arm and kissed her knuckles. "A little shocked, but this is good. This is progress. Is there anything else?"

"It's a first-class ticket. Rosalie once took a bus to Philadelphia to save twenty bucks over the train. I have a hard time believing she'd spring for that by herself." And they knew she'd had partners.

"That camp was pretty nice," Rowe observed.

"Yeah, she's willing to spend money to show off. So was she showing off? Or did she have a rich bene-factor?" She flipped the ticket over to see if there was anything interesting on the back.

It was even better than the front.

Scrawled and smudged, Vi made out two of three handwritten letters.

RS

And then there was part of a phone number. 917 followed by smudges, and ending with 634.

"That's a New York area code," both she and Rowe said at the same time.

"We have to show this to Gibson," he added.

Vi agreed.

But before they could make their next move, there was a knock at the door. "Fuck. That's Owen and Stasia."

"It's okay, this ticket isn't going anywhere." She got up and gave her mate a kiss before answering the door.

Owen was big smiles and engulfed her in a hug that had Rowe growling from deeper in the apart-ment. Stasia was more reserved, but completely polite. They nodded to one another as Vi let them inside.

"What are you looking at?" Owen asked. Rowe hadn't gotten up from the stool. Instead, he'd picked up the ticket stub and was examining it as if it could unlock the secrets of the universe.

"We found a clue," Vi told them. "We'll take it to Gibson once you're back from your luncheon."

"Seems like a good reason to skip," Rowe said as he handed the ticket to Owen.

"You're coming," Stasia commanded. "You owe me. Someone needs to keep *him* in line." She jerked her head at her mate.

"And you trust *him*?" Vi couldn't help but ask.

Stasia shrugged. "Let me see that." She came up beside Owen and looked at the stub. Then she leaned in closer before pulling it out of her mate's hand altogether.

"What is it?" Stasia's face had grown dark.

"He doesn't know about any of this shit. Or he's lying." She was talking to herself, but Owen looked at the paper again and his brow furrowed, as if he was trying to think of something.

"Who?" asked Rowe.

Stasia carefully placed the ticket stub back on the desk. "My brother. AR. Armand Rutherford Selby. ARS. His phone number ends with 634. And he's the one who brought me into contact with Owen."

Owen put an arm around her and tugged her close.

"He never gave me a satisfactory answer to who tried to kidnap me. He said it was something to do with his business. I let it drop. He's shady, it seemed possible. And I was a bit preoccupied with… everything." She leaned into Owen's embrace. "It's only three digits and two initials. It's not proof. But my family has money and ambition. I think it might be time to start asking some hard questions. Fuck the luncheon, let's go talk to Gibson."

"Let me put all this in a folder." Vi had papers scattered everywhere, and there was no way they could take her conspiracy board. A picture of it would have to do for now.

She hoped Rosalie's notes gave them more answers. Her mate deserved to know what had happened to him, and if any more curve balls were coming his way. And she planned to stand at his side and help.

Forever.

EPILOGUE

"You've been working all day, come on." Rowe tugged on his mate's arm, trying to get her away from the desk she'd chained herself to ever since they'd discovered the ticket stub and reported it to Gibson.

"It's not even four," she shot back, not looking up from Rosalie's planner.

"It's four thirty, come on." He pulled just a bit harder and she stood. "We're going out." He handed her a jacket.

"You're going to regret this if we get attacked by evil billionaires while we're out," she said as she grudgingly pulled on the jacket.

Rowe kissed her. "You can protect me."

"Damn straight."

The theater wasn't far and the walk was pleasant, if a little chilly. Rowe held Vi's hand the entire way, and it was hard to believe that a month ago this woman hadn't been in his life and that he hadn't been the kind of man to hold hands while walking down the street.

"Explosions," said his mate.

"What?"

"I want a movie with explosions," she explained. "Stupid and loud and bright."

"I want jokes." He'd seen enough explosions to last several lifetimes, and he was sure more would come their way.

"You're no fun."

"That's not what you said last night." Someone passed by closely enough to bump into her shoulder. "Hey! Watch where you're going!" She looked back and stopped walking. "Nora?"

The shifter looked different than the last time he'd seen her. She'd lost weight and her face was gaunt and sickly. Her hair was greasy, and she looked like she should be in a hospital, not walking down a street.

She blinked a few times before recognition lit in her eyes. "Oh. Vi. Rowe. Hello." Her voice was stronger than he would have expected from the look of her.

"Are you alright?" Vi asked. "Is this—"

"I'm fine. I'm handling it. I have to go." She turned and sped off, knocking into someone else but staying on her feet.

"Should we go after her?" Rowe asked.

"She's a big girl, we can't give her help if she doesn't want it." But it took Vi several more seconds before she could turn away.

They made it to the movie theater, but both the comedy and the explosion movie were sold out.

"What's *Wolf Moon*?" Rowe asked as he looked at the posters for available movies.

"It's so good!" the person at the ticket counter gushed. "These evil werewolves are stalking this village and a bunch of witches have to fight them off. But it's also like a commentary on stuff."

"Stuff?" Vi asked. She looked so skeptical that Rowe had to bite his lip to keep from bursting out laughing.

The ticket person nodded enthusiastically, her eyes bright. "Yeah, like, on the economy. And religion."

"Oh." Vi stepped back and tugged him along. "That sounds terrible," she said, quietly enough that they weren't overheard.

"We can see one of the other movies later," Rowe offered. He had a plan, damn it. This was supposed to be date night.

"Or we could go home and have sex."

Screw the plan.

"Hell yes. What are we standing around here for?"

Vi laughed and Rowe leaned down and kissed

her, pulling her into his embrace and enjoying the feeling of rightness that came with holding his mate.

Thank you for reading Stalking Magic!
I'd appreciate it so much if you would consider leaving a review.

WHAT'S TO READ NEXT: THE ALPHA HEIST

The alpha keeps what's his...

No one steals from Luke Torres. His fortress is legend and his pack of lions are deadly, ready to face any threat. When Luke meets Mel, she knocks his socks off with a scorching kiss, but when they meet again, they are captor and captive in a deadly game of cat vs. cat.

The thief is up to the task...

From the moment Mel takes the assignment, she knows that it should be impossible. But for the supernatural world's foremost thief, impossible is an irresistible challenge. Especially when the payment for this job will get her one step closer to revenge. When the jobs goes belly up, she finds herself in the lion's den and facing off with the most alluring man she's ever met.

Can she find a way to complete the job without losing her heart?

ALSO BY KATE RUDOLPH

Looking for something else? Kate Rudolph has a heart pounding collection or paranormal and sci-fi romance stories for you! Bundles, bears, audiobooks, aliens, and more. Check out your options in the list below. You can find out all you need to know at www.katerudolph.net.

Want to check out one of the books? Click on the series name to find out more!

Zulir Warrior Mates

Kidnapped humans. Alien Warriors. Electric wings.

The Zulir Warrior Mates series brings you human heroines and heroes abducted from Earth who find love – and wings! – with the alien warriors who rescue them.

Also available in audio!

Synnr's Saint

Synnr's Hope

Synnr's Spark

Synnr's Kiss

———

Guarded by the Shifter

Werewolf. Bodyguard. Mate.

The origins of these shifters are shrouded in mystery, but they're determined to protect their mates from any harm that comes their way.

Also available in audio!

Hunting Season

On the Prowl

Stalking Magic

―――――

Detyen Warriors

Detya was destroyed a hundred years ago. These doomed warriors are out to find justice… and their mates.

The Detyen Warriors series brings you kick butt heroines, alpha alien heroes, fated mates, and relationships strong enough to span the galaxy!

The entire series is also available in audio!

Soulless

Ruthless

Heartless

Faultless

Endless

―――――

Alien Holiday Romance

Christmas… in space????

These alien holiday romances look beyond Earth's winter holidays and ring in the season across the galaxy! *Select titles available in audio.*

Snowed in with the Alien Beast

The Alien's Winter Gift

The Alien Reindeer's Wild Ride

Trapped with her Alien Mate

———

Alien Outlaws

Outlaws, schemes, and love… it's all there in the Alien Outlaws series…

Andie Munster is sick of life on Ixilta, the planet she got dumped on after being abducted from Earth six years ago. And when the mysterious and dangerous Xandr shows up looking for a way off the planet, she's half-prisoner, half-co-conspirator in a wild rush to escape.

Rogue Alien's Escape

Rogue Alien's Woman

Rogue Alien's Secret

Rogue Alien's Legacy

———

Mated to the Alien

Fated Mate Alien Romance

Detyens are doomed to die young if they don't find their fated mates.

Follow along as these mated pairs fight off aliens, corrupt dictators, prejudiced humans, pirates, and more! The books can be read or listened to in any order, though some characters show up in multiple stories.

Select books available in audio.

Pick a book and jump into the action today!

Ruwen

Tyral

Stoan

Cyborg

Krayter

Kayleb

Shayn

Braxtyn

Doryan

Dekon

Stealing the Alpha

The thief takes what she wants, but the alpha keeps what's his...

Join shifter thief Mel as she clashes with lion alpha Luke in an explosive trilogy of two opposites who can't keep away from one another.

Also available in audio!

The Alpha Heist

Entangled with the Thief

In the Alpha's Bed

———

Save with box sets!

Aliens. Shifters. Warriors. Mates. Get them all wrapped together in these special box sets. Save up to 30% off the price of buying the individual books, depending on the series!

Alien Outlaws: The Complete Series

Mated to the Alien Volume One (also available in audio)

Mated to the Alien Volume Two (also available in audio)

Mated to the Alien Volume Three

Mated to the Alien Volume Four

Stealing the Alpha: The Complete Series (also available in audio)

The Mate Bundle

Detyen Warriors Volume One (also available in audio)

Detyen Warriors Volume Two (also available in audio)

Standalone Paranormal and Sci-Fi Romance:

Crashed

Mated on the Moon

Mated to the Alien Dragon

Marked

Bear in Mind

Alpha's Mercy

Gemma's Mate

Find more by Kate Rudolph at www.katerudolph.net

ABOUT KATE RUDOLPH

Kate Rudolph is a paranormal and alien romance author who lives in Indiana. She loves writing about kick butt heroines and the steamy heroes who love them. She's been devouring romance novels since she was too young to be reading them and had to hide her books so no one would take them away. She couldn't imagine a better job in this world than writing romances and sharing them with her fellow readers.

If you enjoyed this story, please consider leaving a review.

www.ingramcontent.com/pod-product-compliance
Lightning Source LLC
Chambersburg PA
CBHW010843190726
48286CB00012BA/2965